Rising Above Shepherdsville

Rising
Above
Shepherdsville

Ann Schoenbohm

Beach Lane Books

New York London Toronto Sydney New Delhi

BEACH LANE BOOKS

An imprint of Simon & Schuster Children's Publishing Division

1230 Avenue of the Americas, New York, New York 10020

BEACH LANE BOOKS is a trademark of Simon & Schuster, Inc.

For information about special discounts for bulk purchases, please contact Simon & Schuster Special Sales at 1-866-506-1949 or business@simonandschuster.com.

The Simon & Schuster Speakers Bureau can bring authors to your live event. For more information or to book an event, contact the Simon & Schuster Speakers Bureau at 1-866-248-3049 or visit our website at www.simonspeakers.com.

Jacket design by Sonia Chaghatzbanian

Interior design by Vikki Sheatsley

The text for this book was set in Goudy Oldstyle.

Manufactured in the United States of America

0619 FFG

First Edition

2 4 6 8 10 9 7 5 3 1

Library of Congress Cataloging-in-Publication Data

Names: Schoenbohm, Ann, author.

Title: Rising above Shepherdsville / Ann Schoenbohm.

Description: First edition. | New York : Beach Lane Books, [2019] | Summary: "In 1977, after her mother's suicide, twelve-year-old Dulcie Louise Dixon is sent to live with her aunt and must rise out of her grief and find her voice again with the help of some surprising new friends"— Provided by publisher.

Identifiers: LCCN 2016048802 | ISBN 9781481452830 (hardback) | ISBN 9781481452854 (e-book)

Subjects: | CYAC: Grief—Fiction. | Mothers and daughters—Fiction. | Suicide—Fiction. | Aunts—Fiction. | BISAC: JUVENILE FICTION / Social Issues / Death & Dying. | JUVENILE FICTION / Social Issues / Emotions & Feelings. | JUVENILE FICTION / Social Issues / Suicide.

Classification: LCC PZ7.1.S33652 Ri 2019 | DDC [Fic]—dc23

LC record available at https://lccn.loc.gov/2016048802

For my mother,
Kathryn E. Hannebaum
"pins"

1

f-i-r-m-a-m-e-n-t

firmament (n.)

the sky, viewed poetically as a solid arch or vault

There I was, Mama, standing in the tall grass right next to Redeemer Baptist Church, the day after the Fourth of July, when I spied what I would have sworn on a heap of Bibles was an angel rising straight up to heaven. Enormous white wings spread and soared above me in a sunset so pink and gold, it promised miracles—even here in Shepherdsville, Ohio—a place badly in need of divine intervention, if you ask me.

I never imagined in all my life I'd end up there—the tail end of nowhere without even a Kmart in sight. If I'd had my druthers, Mama, I'd have stayed at home in Paint Creek at Lilac Trailer Court, but I couldn't have said a thing about it, even if I'd wanted to. At the beginning of

June, Ray dumped me at the farm with Aunt Bernie, like a stray pup without a basket.

Ray's caterwauling about ditching me started a few weeks after you'd been gone. He'd gotten in the habit of parking me for days at his mom's house while he was on the road. Old Shirleen didn't have a say in it one way or the other either. She did her best—fed me stale-bread bologna sandwiches and Kool-Aid, trying without success to get me interested in *Days of our Lives* and *General Hospital*, fiddling with the rabbit ears wrapped in tinfoil on top of her old black-and-white TV.

One night Ray showed up, downright pie-eyed. He stumbled up Shirleen's front steps and accidentally yanked the screen door off her house. He stared at that screen door like it had up and bit him, Mama.

"I am fed up trying to fix things, Dulcie."

He laid his wobbly head down on Shirleen's old dinette table and just gave up on me.

"I'm not your daddy, by God, so I can't be responsible for you no more. You'd be better off with your own relations."

Ray packed up the trailer on Lilac Court the next day. He moved his stuff to Shirleen's house. Then he put your knickknacks in boxes, along with your clothes, and sent them to the Salvation Army. He hauled me out to the truck cab, my jeans and T-shirts packed in your old suit-case. He strapped Maybelle to the rear, her rusty spokes and handlebars poking out every which way, then loaded my first-place tri-county spelling bee trophy, along with my dictionary, into a Kroger bag and tossed it behind the driver's seat.

He tucked the small wooden box with the brass plaque—LITTLETON FUNERAL HOME—between us on the seat and drove me to Shepherdsville in a thunderstorm, smoking Kools, while I looked out the window at endless cornfields, hoping he'd change his mind. I thought about what Ray had said about not being my daddy, how he couldn't be responsible for me, and that I'd be better off someplace else. I wish I could have told him he was wrong on all counts. First off—though he wasn't my daddy, he'd done a pretty good imitation of it for almost my whole life. Second—even if he wasn't around as much as we wanted him to be, Mama, he always showed up to fix my bike tires, or make the best grilled cheese sandwiches, or if I'd had a bad day, cheer me up with a dumb joke and make me laugh so hard milk would shoot out my nose. Ray is the definition of responsible. Third, and most important of all—I knew I wasn't going to be better off at Aunt Bernie's farm. I didn't know her from a stray cat. But I did know Ray. I knew he wasn't going to change his mind and he wasn't going to say another word. The only sound for a hundred miles was the squawking of his CB radio and the *thunk-thunk-thunk* of the windshield wipers.

When I showed up with Ray, first thing Aunt Bernie did—after looking me up and down like I'd fallen off a manure truck—was hand me a Bible and start a crusade for my soul—church every Sunday and Bible reading every night. She also threw in housecleaning, dish washing, and feeding the hogs, for good measure. I guess Aunt Bernie imagined it couldn't *hurt* my chances at the Pearly Gates if I had suffered the burden of manual labor, in addition to having spiritual guidance.

Owing to her close personal relationship with the Lord, she figured I'd be a shoo-in with the Almighty if she dropped me off at Redeemer Baptist twice weekly in the evenings, for what has become my own personal abomination on this earth—Reverend Love's Youth Bible Study Group.

Surrounded by endless talk about heaven and the hereafter, it's no wonder I imagined an angel in the sky that night. According to Reverend Love, back in biblical times angels popped up like weeds all the time, appearing to people willy-nilly, here and there, with some kind of proclamation or other.

I didn't expect one would show up in Shepherdsville, next to a dirt parking lot—smack in the middle of nowhere—in 1977, to deliver a message to a twelve-going-on-thirteen-year-old girl. Nope, I didn't think even President Jimmy Carter could manage an angel on earth in modern times—though, Aunt Bernie suspected it wasn't pure coincidence that the president and Jesus had the same initials.

If I hadn't wandered away in the overgrown patch behind the building to find a cool breeze, wanting to escape the heat for just a minute before my descent into that dingy old church basement and the impending gloom of a long evening of Reverend Love droning on about eternal damnation and sin, I would have missed that swan.

For that's what it was, Mama, only an earthly bird in flight, and not an angel at all. High above the treetops, rising like a rocket shot into the heavens, that majestic creature soared and took my heart along with it. Its wings gleamed, so pure and downy I wanted to reach up and touch them. The ease of that swan as it lifted into the sky made me want to climb aboard its back and fly away—far from Shepherdsville—back home to you, instead of standing by a ditch, next to a rickety church, clutching a raggedy Bible.

Redeemer Baptist probably hasn't changed one iota

since you were a girl, Mama. The church is still a mish-mash of old white clapboards nailed together, leaning every which way. The tired dirt-brown doors hang catawampus, repainted so many times, they don't close right. A rusty brass bell hangs near the entrance, with a long tattered cord that Reverend Love pulls to call us inside to worship. The oversize cross on top of the roof is downright pitiful in its need to call attention to itself, and makes the whole building seem to say, *I know I don't look like a church, but this here cross is proof.*

Knowing you'd stood there, once upon a time, was a comfort. The landscape in front of me was like a faded watercolor: the waving field of patchy grass and poison oak; the weed-infested cemetery; the picnic area sprinkled with rickety tables; the rusty swingset leaning sideways in the gravel; the big oaks standing guard by the edge of the church property, surrounded by endless pasture. At the far end of the field, a broken-down fence with a NO TRESPASS-ING sign invited brave souls who might dare cross it.

For the first time in the days since you'd been gone, Mama, something joyful welled up inside me. Maybe it was a trick of the light, but a sliver of water seemed to appear beyond the thicket of trees, like a mirage shimmering in the distance, beckoning me away from there.

The sky hinted of things to come; a tinge of possibility lingered, right there with me. I knew I'd best get inside before Bible study began, but I hesitated, held fast by my desire to rise into the coming night air, right out of my church shoes, held aloft by those giant wings.

Inside the church the choir began their practice for the service come Sunday. A current of air whispered to me, carrying the words of a hymn, their meaning as mysterious as the swan's appearance.

> *Rock of Ages, cleft for me,*
> *Let me hide myself in thee; . . .*
> *When I soar to worlds unknown . . .*

In a few weeks' time, those voices would sing at my baptism—the event that Aunt Bernie and Reverend Love had arranged, Mama, in cahoots with the Lord, to save my soul and cure me of what they called my "affliction."

My silence.

I hadn't spoken a word—not one—since you'd been gone, Mama. Not one sound in over two months. When I was called on to speak, I couldn't. My words had dried up and blown away somewhere, and no matter how hard I looked, I couldn't find them.

After not getting a peep out of me, Ray took me to the mental ward of the Ross County hospital. The nurses gave me little pink pills. When I wasn't sleeping, people in white coats shined lights into my eyes, lodged tongue depressors in my mouth, inserted needles, and wreaked tests upon me for six days, like the deadly plagues in the Bible.

On the seventh day they brought me into an office. Ray sat in a wooden chair holding on to his International Harvester hat, his eyes blinking and twitching when he saw me.

"She's had a trauma," the doctor said. "Take her home."

Then he handed me a small notebook with one of those yellow happy faces on it, and smiled.

"Write down what you want to say." He shook hands with Ray. "Time will take care of it."

Ray walked me out to Shirleen's battered-up station wagon, muttering under his breath. "Time will take care of it, my butt." He jerked the handle, opened the car door, and practically shoved me inside.

He got in and said, "If you don't stop this right now, I am telling you . . ." He gripped the wheel, his knuckles white. "I can't lose my dang job, calling in sick, taking you to doctors all over creation. You need somebody to watch over you proper. I got to go back on the road. Shirleen's too old to help out much. I can't be expected to take care of a girl by myself—especially one who doesn't say a blessed word."

I opened the notebook the doctor had given me and wrote: *Go to H-E-double matchsticks, Ray. You're not the boss of me.* He said I was just stubborn. Maybe I was, because my voice was still on the loose, a runaway that had packed up and left.

Imagine, Mama. Me—winner of the Paint Creek spelling bee, pride of Ross County, tri-county regional winner—washed up. The girl who'd stood in a gymnasium full of people, armed with definitions, pronouncing words as loud as you please—speechless—struck dumb.

Dumb—that's what they called me down in that church basement, along with a few other words I don't care to repeat.

"Dumb." *Webster's* definition: "lacking the power of speech."

D-u-m-b.

Even when we didn't have anything else, we always had words, didn't we, Mama? All those nights with the television on the fritz, Ray off trucking somewhere, we traded the big blue *Webster's New World Dictionary* back and forth, warming our feet next to the electric heater, going through the spelling lists, word after word.

We collected the best ones like pretty rocks, looking for the shiniest ones to put in our pockets like precious souvenirs. Those words, you said, were our magic spell against unpaid bills, mac-and-cheese dinners, and the holes in our shoes. You said they would circle us and keep us from wanting: "infinitesimal," "ameliorate," "miraculous," "obsequious," "grandiloquent," "percolate," "bellicose," "mercurial."

Like an incantation, the words conspired to get us out of the trailer court—sail us out of there. You wouldn't have to serve another piece of pie at the Starliner Diner, or worry about Ray carousing at every honky-tonk on Highway 70, because I had a trick bag full of words.

We had a plan, Mama. With those *infinitesimal* words, I'd get a spot at Briarwood Academy, where the rich kids went. With those *miraculous* words, I'd go to college. With those *grandiloquent* words, we'd get out of the trailer court forever.

But you found your own way out of Lilac Court.

Without any warning, I lost you . . . and I lost all the words.

As I watched that swan disappear beyond the trees, my skin pricked into little bumps down my arms. Remember what you always told me, Mama?

Goose bumps are a sign that a thing is true-blue, a way your body tells your mind that something is real and right in front of you.

Nope, there was no angel with a message.

Even if Gabriel himself had come down into the parking lot, stood on a picnic table with a megaphone, and hollered, "Dulcie Louise Dixon, you need saving!" I wouldn't have believed it.

I knew that swan was a sign, Mama. We both know the truth of it. There are some things you can't be saved from.

Nobody was going to save me from that church basement.

Nooo-buddy.

So I put down Aunt Bernie's Bible, and ran.

2

s-a-n-c-t-u-a-r-y

sanctuary (n.)

a holy place; a place of refuge or protection

With no idea what lay ahead, Mama, I followed that swan. My feet sang a hushed song as I swished through the wild grass along the fence line. When I came to the NO TRESPASSING sign at the far corner of the field, I stopped.

I glanced back at the church—not a soul in sight—no sign of Reverend Love. The weathered wood fence lay in pieces on the ground. The lonely cemetery was barely visible from where I stood.

I considered my next move—whether or not to cross to the other side. "Trespassing" was a mighty word in church. Reverend Love prayed every Sunday, *"Forgive us our trespasses, as we forgive those who trespass against us."*

I gathered that curiosity wasn't exactly the same thing as trespassing. Aunt Bernie had pointed out to me that curiosity was why the mouse who kept trespassing in her kitchen had ended up with his tail nipped off. But I figured that old mouse would never get the cheese if he didn't have a sense of adventure. Maybe that was why he kept coming back—he knew that the cost might be worth the risk.

I stepped over to the other side easily, but not before I ripped the new church dress Aunt Bernie had insisted on buying me at Marva's Dress Shop in town.

When I first came to Shepherdsville, she discovered that all I had in my suitcase were jeans and T-shirts. She was horrified. "These will *not* do in the Lord's house," is what she said, her face pursed up like a hundred-year-old prune. She bought me two ugly dresses from Marva's with bows and pouffy sleeves—things I wouldn't wear to a dogfight.

There I was, Mama, the torn hem of my ugly dress hanging down, lopsided, as I picked my way into the wooded thicket past the fence line. Tiny burrs attached and burrowed into my knee socks. My hands stung from nettle scratches as I pushed my way through the overgrowth. Something pulled me forward, tugging me farther into the trees, their mighty trunks circling round like guarding soldiers. Over my shoulder the church disappeared from view.

I pushed past dense weedy patches until I stumbled into a clearing of waist-high stalks and reeds. An enormous weeping willow greeted me, long tendrils dancing before me in the sun. Cattails and wild irises hid a treasure—the sliver of water I had glimpsed from the field behind the church.

It wasn't a real pond, more like a marshy green teardrop fixing to dry up, surrounded by bulrushes and shoots of tall field grasses. If I took good aim, I probably could have landed a rock on the other side—that's how small it was. It was hard to tell where the water began and the earth stopped. A mounded nest of twigs and leaves rose on the uppermost branches of a fallen tree limb in the middle—creating a tiny makeshift island—big enough for Lilliputians, not sturdy enough for my Gulliver-size feet.

Breathless from running, my heart thumping hard, I put my hand on my chest, still half-fearful Reverend Love might have seen me run off. I stood, motionless, waiting for my breath to return to normal.

Like magic, two white swans glided past on the far side of the pond. They grazed along the bank, pulling reeds out of the shallows. They seemed to be waiting for me, like creatures out of a fairy tale, skimming the water, with their snow-white feathers and impossibly long necks curved into S's. Their eyes gleamed, outlined in glistening black. Dipping here and there, their orange beaks glinted in the setting sun.

Five little ones followed the bigger swans in perfect order, scrambling not to be left behind. Their bodies sprouted light-gray downy feathers tinged with yellow-brown edges. I moved closer, careful not to disturb them. A twisted limb slanted off a gnarled tree, a perfect seat for me to watch them at their family business. I climbed up onto it and sat with my back against the trunk, legs outstretched, captivated.

The swans seemed to have a natural language all their own. The babies responded to each movement of the bigger swans with little pecks and shoves. Their tiny wings unfurled like boat sails when they got riled. They pulled and tugged at one another, each movement full of meaning. The only sounds were little rustles of the water they disturbed.

Immediately I felt as if I understood them and as if they understood me, too.

As I watched them gliding on the surface of the water, I finally understood that poem Mrs. Whitehouse made us recite last year about how the beauty of the world is in the smallest things. Most of all, I remembered how it felt to let the words float effortlessly, like dust motes in the classroom.

> To see a World in a Grain of Sand
> And a Heaven in a Wild Flower
> Hold Infinity in the palm of your hand
> And Eternity in an hour

I wished I could have recited it again, letting my voice flow as freely as you please. But I only made breathy whispers when I tried, my lips forming the words, my body refusing to help my voice make sound. I was drowning in a pool of unspoken words, their weight keeping me silent altogether.

Imagining you were right beside me helped. All I had to do was pretend we were sitting on the front stoop of the trailer at Lilac Court, or dangling our feet out at the lake.

You always said if we looked hard enough, there are bits of heaven right here on this earth. This place felt like that for me—a place where I wasn't expected to talk— where nobody wanted to cure me, where nobody stared at me like I was damaged goods. I wasn't stuck in a hot basement with a crop of homegrown farm boys with cowlicks in their hair and manure on their shoes, or mean holier-than-thou girls who wore pretty dresses and ugly stares, who meowed under their breath, "Cat got your tongue?" or whispered just loud enough for me to hear, "Are you crazy? Crazy like your mama?"

Their words prickled like thorns. Stuck in my craw but good. But I understood how people could get the wrong impression.

"Crazy." *Webster's* definition: "having flaws or cracks; shaky or rickety; unsound."

C-r-a-z-y l-i-k-e y-o-u-r m-a-m-a.

Ray told me you were baking cookies, of all things.

The morning after he accidentally ripped the screen door off Shirleen's house, he made me eggs for breakfast. He didn't say a word about taking me to Shepherdsville. I figured he'd forgotten what he'd said: *"I'll be staying with Shirleen from now on. I'm driving you to Bernie's farm tomorrow, first thing."*

He stood at the stove, red-eyed, staring at the pan in front of him. His voice was gravelly, as if he were coughing up pebbles.

"Listen, I know you've got questions, Dulcie."

Well, Mama, he had that right.

He broke eggs, poured in the milk.

I sat at the dinette booth and looked out at the court. The flagpole out front rose to the sky, surrounded at the base by drooping petunias that hadn't been watered in days. All the trailers sat grouped in a circle, giving the impression they were eavesdropping on Ray's every word.

He whipped the eggs into a froth with a fork.

"She'd had a hard time of it when I met her. You know that."

He told me the story of how he met you, Mama, how he'd seen you at the Starliner, balancing burgers and fries like an acrobat in the circus. "She was something else, your mama." When Ray found out we were living at the YWCA and that you were paying most of your paycheck to a babysitter for me, he brought you to his mama's house. He told me how he and Shirleen took us in, cared for you and me, like we were family. Later, when he'd bought the trailer at Lilac Court for us to live in, you'd kept on paying him rent. "She insisted on that. Didn't want to be dependent on nobody." Ray's voice got soft. "But now, things gotta change, girl. I'm sorry. I gotta do what's right by you. Your mama never meant . . ." His words trailed off.

Swirling some butter around in the pan, Ray poured in the eggs, then leaned on the counter.

I picked at my thumbnail. There was a rip there, and I dug at it.

Ray cleared his throat.

"It was an accident, Dulce. She was making cookies, is all. She probably wanted to surprise you. A congratulations for doing well at the spelling bee. She knew you'd win, don't ya see? She believed in you, ya know."

Ray's eyes never left the eggs, not one glance my way. He seemed to be telling himself, not me.

I wanted to ask, "*Well, if she was baking cookies, what kind were they, Ray? Chocolate chip? Oatmeal? And how come a woman who never so much as baked a cake a day in her life, all of a sudden got it into her head to whip up a batch of baked goods, like she was Betty Crocker?*"

"She turned the oven on, probably to preheat it— most likely didn't even know that the pilot light wasn't lit. Hardly used the thing, as it was."

I leaned back and put my feet up under me. I wrapped my arms and legs like I was ready to cannonball into the lake.

I could hear the *scrape-scrape* of a fork against the pan as Ray piled the eggs onto a plate.

"It was an accident, is all. You know she'd been tired, working so many shifts. She just laid down to get some shut-eye before work. She only meant to nap."

I tried to imagine what he was saying, Mama. I thought of you lying down, curled up on the couch, the old crocheted afghan over you, breathing, and then—not.

In my mind's eye I watched myself tell Mrs. Whitehouse to turn the car around, *take me home*, I wasn't going to the spelling bee, listening to the voice inside telling me, *Something's wrong, something's wrong*. But I didn't do that, Mama. If I had just listened to myself—opened my mouth—then I could have saved you. I would have pulled the blanket off, opened the windows, slapped your face and shouted, *Mama, Mama*, loud enough for you to hear and come back to me.

"It was just an accident," Ray said again, putting the eggs in front of me.

I left the eggs on the table and walked out the door, making sure it slammed. That was when he started packing my things.

He could say it all he wanted. But he had it all wrong.

It was my fault. I was the one who left you alone.

3

c-e-l-e-s-t-i-a-l
celestial (adj.)
of the heavens; of the sky; divine

The church bell clanged in the distance—Reverend Love pulling the long cord by the front doors, calling us in to Bible study. No matter how much I wanted to stay put right where I was, Mama, I knew I'd best get back before somebody figured out I was missing. Reverend Love would be sure to call Aunt Bernie, who would be madder than a wet hen in a bucket.

I made my way back through the clearing. The swans ignored me; they were clustered together near the center of the pond, busy preening. The lowering sun made it hard for me to see as I wandered back to the church through the trees. I climbed back over the fence and scurried to the rear of the building like a jackrabbit. My shoes squelched, soggy from the spongy earth near the pond, my knees were muddy, and my dress hem was in tatters.

Winded, I rounded the corner to the picnic area. The Bible that Aunt Bernie had given me was right where I'd left it.

Reverend Love appeared in front of me, causing me to nearly jump out of my knee socks. He leaned his head sideways, his glasses filmy with the heat, observing me with a look that I couldn't say was good or bad. He squinted at me and cupped his eyes against the fading sun, searching the trees beyond.

"Dulcie, there you are. I wondered what had become of you."

His eyes crinkled under his shaggy brows. "Come on out of there, so I don't have to explain to Bernice how you got chiggers down your socks." He stepped toward me, reaching out his hands like Jesus in the picture on the wall above Aunt Bernie's television set.

Reverend Love loped his way nearer, his long rubbery limbs not cooperating with the rest of his body. He was basketball-player-tall and young enough to sprout pimples from time to time. There was a faint scar across his right cheek that made him look fierce, when he didn't look downright bewildered. Aunt Bernie said he was wet behind the ears but meant well. She told me the congregation was still settling in with him—fresh out of divinity college with newfangled ideas about how to run a church.

On Sundays people would stand around in clumps, their arms crossed, whispering about the sermon, clucking like chickens. I'd overheard folks gossiping that Reverend Love had been in jail for robbing a gas station before he was a preacher. Aunt Bernie said people talked nonsense. She let me know right off she thought that Reverend Love was a bright star in a dark world. She hung on his every word as if he could unhook the moon and bring it right down to earth.

He seemed harmless to me, more like a pretend preacher than the imposing type I imagined the Lord would set forth in the world to keep the peace and save the sinners. Reverend Love certainly couldn't control that wild pack down in the church basement on Tuesday and Thursday nights.

So I doubted he felt threatened by a girl who never said a word to him. Reverend Love inspected me further, his expression as unreadable as the Sphinx in Egypt, surveying the condition of my dress and my dirty knees. He shifted his head sideways and nodded out to the woods beyond the church cemetery.

"I've been told there's a swan's nest back in there

somewhere." The corner of his mouth rose the slightest bit. "But I don't think anyone ever goes there."

Quiet for a moment, he pushed his glasses back up onto the bridge of his nose, avoiding asking directly where I'd been—though clearly, he had an inkling. "Probably best to keep that a secret between you and me."

His eyes met mine, and I nodded. He considered the sky then, his face softening. He didn't act particularly eager to get to Bible study either. "One of the poets, I forget which, said that swans ferry souls to heaven."

Despite the warm evening, a chill danced up my arms. The strange miracle of the swan leading me to a secret place that no one knew about—except Reverend Love and me— crackled, electric and unspoken between us. We stood by the patchy field as the sky deepened into a darker blue.

He lowered his head as if he meant to pray right there. "Some things remain hidden until they are meant to be seen."

The field suddenly seemed to buzz alive with sound, the night bugs and cicadas gearing up for the night ahead, making such a ruckus, my ears rang.

"Do you ever read poetry?" he asked.

I shook my head. I had no way to tell him, Mama, how we used to read Robert Frost poems and Shakespeare sonnets aloud at night.

Reverend Love looked at his shoes and put his hands in his pockets. "When I was younger and had time on my hands, I read poetry every day." I wondered if he was referring to his supposed stint in the slammer.

He looked into the distance, his gaze faraway. "I read once that cicadas are the souls of dead poets, and the sounds they make are lamentations for all the words they meant to write. Lost poetry waiting to be heard . . ." He trailed off, lost in his thoughts.

My eyes felt hot. The song of the coming night was louder and more insistent. Something about the way Reverend Love spoke made me consider the words I'd wanted for myself. Words from you, Mama, that I never got.

After you were gone, Mama, I tore the trailer apart looking for some word from you—a note, anything. I looked in every cabinet, pulled out drawers, tossed cushions off the couch—nothing, not one word. I wanted to believe you'd just gone to the store, or were at work, that I'd find something written down, some explanation.

Dulcie, went to the laundromat. Do your homework. Mac and cheese in the cupboard. Big love, Mama.

But you packed up all the words and took them with you and left only longing in their place—a permanent knot in my throat that wouldn't come undone. As I stood next to Reverend Love, the dark field spread out before us, I imagined I could sing along with those heat bugs, join in their humming choir of longing.

Reverend Love smacked at a mosquito. A tiny dot of blood spotted his white shirt sleeve. Whether it was the stain on his shirt or the passing of the mosquito, something appeared to sadden him.

Reverend Love took in a long breath, pulling air deep into his lungs. He seemed as reluctant as I was to leave the deepening sky and the possibility of the heavens. He motioned toward the open door of the church. "We'd best get inside, before we become a feast."

I picked up my Bible from the picnic table and followed him.

At the porch he touched my shoulder, his hand alighting there as if it were a small, steady bird. "Let's have faith that it will go better tonight, shall we? Keep your chin up."

I think he was trying to steel himself as much as give me a pep talk, Mama. Then he led me inside to face the stares and whispers.

As we walked past the sanctuary, the last of the day's light broke into a prism of color through the one stained-glass window above the pulpit. The choir stood gathered around the organ, their voices lifting the air, giving it weight.

In their midst, front and center, a radiant woman led the others in the singing of the hymn. I'd never seen her, or in fact any person like her, in Shepherdsville before. She commanded my attention with her voice and manner, as if she, too, were a vision that had appeared right there in the sanctuary. Her silver hair surrounded her head like a halo, and the church lights threw gold on her brown skin. Her arms reached up to the sky as she sang out. Her voice, powerful and majestic, reached right in and took ahold of my heart.

> Come home, come home;
> ye who are weary, come home;
> earnestly, tenderly, Jesus is calling,
> calling, O sinner, come home!

The organ hummed, soft and low. The choir ended their practice on a high sweet note. As I followed Reverend Love down the rickety stairs to the chair basement meeting room, I held the vision of the swan to me like a prayer, Mama, my heart whispering what my voice could not. *Come back. Come back for me.*

4

r-i-g-h-t-e-o-u-s
righteous (adj.)
morally right; fair and just

Oh, Mama, how I hated that church basement meeting room. It steamed hotter than the devil's own breath. Trapped air and the smell of sweaty armpits mingled, with nowhere to go. The overhead fluorescent bulbs hummed, highlighting the scuffed linoleum and dingy walls. Green metal chairs were corralled in a circle, waiting for us to sit. The church kitchen at the far end of the room reeked of stale coffee and yeasty donuts.

My stomach fluttered as if a nest of birds had been let loose inside me, Mama. I'd survived Bible study enough times to know what was in store and the main culprits who would make misery for me.

Loretta Swinson, Leann Shank, and their crowd

of infidels stood circled around the bench at the piano, mercilessly thumping out a tinny rendition of "Heart and Soul," painful to the ears.

Aunt Bernie often pointed out that the Swinsons were the wealthiest family in Shepherdsville and that they lined the church coffers accordingly. As rich people, they were justifiably snooty, but their daughter, Loretta, had perfected the craft. Her nose was upturned so high, you could count her nostril hairs.

Her friend Leann Shank wore her curly hair pulled so tight in a ponytail, I swear it cut off the circulation to her brain. She followed Loretta around like a caboose and did Loretta's heartless bidding. Missy Spangler, Susie Wickert, and the other girls were equally mindless in their adoration of Loretta. They moved as a pack, mean as garbage hounds.

Jason Burdine, Matt Jensen, Lerman Henckle, and the other boys whooped it up, tossing balled-up bits of newspaper into a metal wastebasket, converting half the room into a makeshift basketball court. They pitched four-letter words according to their failure or success rate.

"Sheet, Burdine, that sucked."

"Sum-beach, Jensen. *You* suck."

Matt Jensen sported muscles from pitching hay and

had a big old crush on Loretta—a pitiful affliction that made him look like a sick puppy. He spent most of his time trying to get her attention.

And Jason, well, he was as mean as his daddy.

Otis Burdine thought nothing of whupping Jason upside the head outside the Lord's house on a Sunday. "Did you hear what I said, boy? I don't want nothing out of your mouth, or I will burn your backside."

Every Sunday the Burdines left their old hunting dog, Marlow, tied up next to their pickup truck in the parking lot. The back window of their old rusty Ford sported two or three hunting rifles on a gun rack, just in case they felt the need to pick off one of God's creatures on the way home from church, I expect.

When Reverend Love wasn't looking, Jason's particular specialty was flicking boogers or the occasional spitball at my face.

Mama, they were a righteous bunch, all right. They not only acted justified in refusing to accept me into their fold, they seemed free of any guilt in their determination to run poor Reverend Love right out of town.

The usual snickers greeted me when I entered the room. Hand-covered mouths whispered farm town gossip, and unkind eyes stared into mine, saying, *You aren't like us.*

My silence seemed to rile them worse than if I had given them a piece of my mind.

Reverend Love clapped his hands for everyone's attention.

"Let's get started, y'all." Reverend Love's Kentucky drawl seemed slower in the basement. No one paid him any mind; he commanded as much attention with that bunch as a common housefly.

He clapped his hands again, his voice wavering.

"Come on, y'all. Join hands."

I stood in the circle, the swan's flight above the church having lifted my heart, making me hopeful that the evening would go according to Reverend Love's plan.

"Let us pray," he said.

My right hand was encased in Jason's sweaty mitt, my left hand clamped in Loretta's cold bony grip.

Reverend Love lowered his head.

"Dear Lord, we ask you to help us tonight as we study your Good Book. Enable us to embrace your word and one another. Let us do unto one another as we would have done to us. Let us look into our hearts and forgive one another our transgressions. . . ."

Reverend Love let out a big poof of air.

"And we need rain, Lord. It's hot. A drop or two would

be most appreciated. In your name we pray. Amen."

When we were done with the prayer, Jason and Loretta dropped my hands like they were burning coals of fire.

Reverend Love adjusted his glasses. Little beads of sweat peppered his forehead. The jerky motion of the nearby fan didn't cool us a whit. He mopped his face with a hanky from his pocket.

"Tonight I want to talk about sin."

He looked at Jason. "Jason, what is sin?"

Jason looked at his feet and mumbled something.

"Speak up, Jason."

Jason slumped lower in his chair. "I don't know. Breaking the law."

Matt threw his hand up, his eyes on Loretta. "Fornication is a sin."

With the mention of the f-word, the room erupted. One of the other farm boys, Carl, called out, "Thinking about it is a sin too, Jensen."

There was all manner of hoots and knee slapping.

Reverend Love's face went red. "Pipe down, y'all. Come on, now."

Missy Spangler rocked in her seat, back and forth, thinking so hard, her eyes screwed up. She burst out, "Ooh. Ooh, Reverend Love. I know. Is it . . . ? Um . . ."

We waited for the end of time while she searched through the empty spaces of her mind.

Reverend Love decided to have pity on us. "Breaking a commandment?"

"Yeah, that's what I was gonna say," Missy said, and beamed with pride.

Reverend Love gave her a weak smile. He looked around at all of us. "Other ideas about sin?"

Loretta, as perky as a parakeet, always tweet-tweeting to be the center of attention, sat up straighter in her chair next to me and raised her hand.

"Reverend Love?"

"Yes?"

Loretta smoothed her skirt, then deliberately wound one long red curl around her finger. She stared at me like I was a curious bug she'd uncovered and was ready to squash.

"What about what Dulcie's mother did? Doesn't a person who does that go straight to hell?"

She looked innocently at Reverend Love as if she'd eaten a cream puff, smug satisfaction in her eyes. She was quite pleased with herself.

Quite pleased.

Until I hit her smack on the head with my Bible.

5

t-r-a-n-s-g-r-e-s-s

transgress (n.)

to step over, pass over; to go beyond

Loretta grabbed the top of her head, her eyes so wide, I thought they'd pop out. Neither one of us moved. I don't know who was more shocked, Mama—me or Loretta. Reverend Love's mouth was a big round cavern. An "oh" escaped from it, before all measure of commotion broke loose. Everyone jumped to their feet, chairs clattering to the floor in a jumble of clanking metal and loud shouts.

Missy Spangler bawled like a baby in all the ruckus due to Loretta having accidentally hit her in the eye with an elbow. Matt Jensen shook his fist at me. Jason hooted. The other boys chanted, "Fight. Fight. Fight," egging Loretta to hit me back. Eventually Loretta hollered—a delayed reflex kicking into the cerebral cortex of her pea-size brain.

"Ow!"

Then she said it again in such a way that suggested she hadn't gotten it right the first time. "OW!" She continued on like that as though she were stuck. "Ow. Ow. Ow. Ow."

Reverend Love raised his voice to be heard over all of it.

"Stop it, y'all. Right now."

Nobody heard him. He picked up one of the metal chairs and banged it on the floor so hard, it caused an echo. We clapped our hands over our ears in unison.

He roared as if he were Moses parting the waters with the power of his voice.

"Sit down. All of y'all. Now!"

Everyone froze—a game of statues with Bibles.

Reverend Love waited, breathing hard, his face dripping wet as if he'd run through a sprinkler. He struck me as being surprised at himself. Maybe he hadn't known he had it in him to take charge until that very moment. He appeared to be satisfied, giving the impression that he'd wanted to yell that way for a good long time.

He boomed like thunder, enjoying himself thoroughly, "Now, open your Bibles, shut your mouths up, and . . ."

He seemed at a loss momentarily, then sputtered,

"Memorize the books of the Old Testament in order." He paused. "Then in reverse order. Whoever doesn't know 'em, gets pew duty."

Pew duty meant wiping up the pews after church on Sunday, a job nobody wanted. Wiping up that particular sticky residue of sweat, prayer, and heat was not for the fainthearted.

"Dulcie, come with me."

I followed Reverend Love back up the rickety stairs to the main floor by the entry hall, off the main doors. The church office was deserted except for ancient Mrs. Bushnell, who was typing up church bulletins. Reverend Love went directly to the watercooler, filled up a little paper cone of water, gulped it down, filled another, and gave it to me. He led me to a bench by the front doors, sat, and patted the spot next to him. I sat down, balancing the water, trying not to spill.

"Well, that didn't go so well, did it?"

I shook my head and gulped my water.

"Look, I know Loretta intended to get under your skin. But I can't have you hitting anybody, plain and simple. Even if they are asking for it." He poked the tattered carpet with his toe.

"Y'all will have to ask each other for forgiveness, you hear?"

I shrugged. The voice in my head answered him straight from Kentucky, loud and clear: *Y'all will have to wait until the second coming before that happens.*

"Come on, now. We can get along if we try, can't we?"

My shoulders stuck in a permanent hunch. If I had to lay eyes on Loretta again, I'd spit up blood.

"I have faith in you, Dulcie."

The inability to tell him not to waste his faith made me crumple the paper cone cup into a little ball and squeeze it hard.

Reverend Love patted my knee, then got up from the bench.

"I'll have Mrs. Bushnell give Bernice a call to come get you. I think that's best, don't you?"

I wanted to tell him that he might as well drive me to purgatory and drop me off.

"You go on and wait outside till your aunt arrives. I best get back downstairs before somebody burns the place down." He paused. "I'll have a talk with Loretta after Bible study about her remark."

Reverend Love headed into the office, then stopped in the doorway. He leaned out, holding the doorframe with one hand.

"Dulcie." He looked over the top of his glasses. "I know

you might not think so, but the Bible *does* come in handy sometimes." The side of his face lifted, a sly hint of a grin threatening his seriousness.

I couldn't help but smile at that. He really wasn't so bad, Mama, considering he was a preacher. Reverend Love and I had an unspoken agreement, it seemed, to look out for each other. We were both on the same end of the stick with that crowd downstairs, and besides, we shared the secret of the swan's nest.

After he went back downstairs, I opened the front doors and wandered outside, glad to be free of the church.

Lightning bugs twinkled, tiny sparks in the darkened fields around me. I sat on the concrete church steps and watched for Aunt Bernie's headlights, my stomach tight.

I couldn't explain to her that I'd had to stick up for you, Mama, about you not being a sinner.

About it all being my fault.

I couldn't explain to Aunt Bernie how it had been, the night before the spelling finals, when you'd helped me practice my spelling list and I'd gotten stuck on the word "premonition."

You seemed so tired, Mama, when you squinted at the list.

"'Premonition.' You know this one."

"*P-r-e-m-i* . . ."

"We've gone over this list twenty times, Dulcie. You know this. Start over."

"Mama, I don't have to go."

"Of course you do," you said. "Now, come on. We need that trophy. I'll put it next to the other one at the Starliner, along with your picture. Briarwood Academy will have no choice but to give a scholarship to a girl who's got two trophies under her belt."

You'd mailed the application the day before, and we both knew it was a long shot for a scholarship. Briarwood took only one scholarship student a year, but that didn't stop you from acting like it was a sure thing.

"*P-r-e-m-e-n* . . ."

But no matter how many times I tried that night, it wouldn't come to me.

When I came to Shepherdsville, I had no way to tell Aunt Bernie that if I hadn't gotten into the car with Mrs. Whitehouse to go to state finals—if I hadn't left you alone—if instead I'd gone back and stayed with you—if only I'd done that, Mama, you wouldn't have turned on the oven to bake those cookies Ray insisted you were aiming to make.

"Premonition." *Webster's* definition: "a feeling that something bad will happen; a forewarning."

After you were gone, Mama, the spelling came to me with no trouble at all. I just couldn't say it out loud.

Aunt Bernie pulled her car into the parking lot of the church, the sound of her wheels on the gravel like a giant munching boulders. She drove up to the steps where I sat, creeping toward me, cutting her headlights as she came nearer.

In the yellow glare from the light on the telephone pole, I could make out Aunt Bernie's posture—I could tell from the set of her head and the way her hands gripped the wheel that I was in for a night of crossed arms and pursed lips.

P-r-e-m-o-n-i-t-i-o-n.

Could Aunt Bernie even understand how things were at Lilac Court? That Ray and me had to watch out for you sometimes, when you'd get sad? Would she understand that Ray had every right to dump me in Shepherdsville? If only I'd told him about you, things might have been different. How could I explain that I didn't tell Ray because he'd been driving weeks of back-to-back long hauls? That I didn't want to bother him? I could tell he was tired of it, Mama. Tired of trying to make things better. I needed him to think things were okay with you.

I should have told Ray how you didn't laugh much

anymore, Mama—how you slept all the time when you weren't at work, or hardly ate—how I'd wake up in the middle of the night and hear you cry out. But every time Ray came home, I pretended nothing was wrong.

I couldn't explain to Aunt Bernie that I did what you told me to do that last morning, rather than listen to the voice in my head that said, *Stay. Don't you leave her alone.* I walked straight out the screen door and got into Mrs. Whitehouse's car and headed off to win that trophy.

How could I tell her the worst thing of all, Mama?

That when Mrs. Whitehouse asked if that was my mother who'd come out onto the steps, in her robe, waving, blowing me a kiss, I pretended I didn't hear, and just continued telling Joann Benson what Nelson Lenderman had said on the bus the day before, like it was the most important thing in the world? That I didn't look out the window at you and wave back?

How could Aunt Bernie understand why I didn't look back? Or understand that when Mrs. Whitehouse's car turned out of Lilac Court that morning, the spelling of the word "premonition" was easy on my tongue, the definition repeating in my head.

"Premonition": "a feeling that something bad will happen; a forewarning."

I walked across the gravel of Redeemer's parking lot to Aunt Bernie's car, carrying my Bible close to my chest like a shield, even though I knew it wouldn't help me explain a darn thing. Before I slid into the front seat, I looked up at the starless sky, the memory of the swan rising into the heavens now replaced with darkness.

6

r-e-q-u-i-e-s-c-a-t

requiescat (n.)

a prayer for the repose of the dead

Aunt Bernie didn't say a word the whole way back to the farm, Mama. She played the radio, music from WGOD—the religious radio station transmitting from a small white house at the edge of town with a miniature tower perched in the front yard. She did the station's accounting twice a week and always had it tuned in while she was in the kitchen or in her car.

When the farm report came on, interrupting the gospel music, she switched to a news station. Her finger pushed the buttons under the dial as if she wanted to poke somebody in the eye. I rolled down the window and let my arm float in the breeze.

The newscaster's voice spilled out into the night as

we passed through town. Some guy with a complicated name had taken over the country of Pakistan, and the Cincinnati Reds had won their baseball game against the Atlanta Braves. After the sports, Aunt Bernie switched the radio off.

We drove through Shepherdsville in silence. The one stoplight in town gleamed red, a silent eye in the night. Everything was closed up tight, windows dark, empty sidewalks—a ghost town, except for me and Aunt Bernie.

We turned onto Victory Road, the world around us flat, except for the rising corn whispering alongside us. All the land on this road had belonged to us Dixons for a hundred years, Aunt Bernie told me, but she had sold off parcels over the years, so she could keep the farmhouse. Since I had your last name, Mama, knowing that this part of Shepherdsville had once belonged to our family made it seem precious, something besides our names that connected me and you and Aunt Bernie.

The farmhouse where you grew up, surrounded by an endless ocean of cornstalks and soybeans, seemed like a tiny island isolated from the rest of Shepherdsville. I couldn't see why Aunt Bernie stayed there by herself, Mama. It seemed like the loneliest place on earth, but I had to admit, it was strangely beautiful in its way.

The day Ray drove me there, I woke up from a nap in the truck cab and felt transported, like Dorothy to the Land of Oz, when they changed the scene to technicolor on the television. The greens seemed greener and the sky hung right above our heads, a tint of blue that I'd only seen in a crayon box. It certainly was far from anyplace that hinted at civilization, like a proper Kroger or a Sunoco station or even a White Castle.

Ray blew out a puff of smoke and gestured with his arm, taking in all the expanse around us.

"Welcome to God's country."

He didn't appear to have much regard for it—he flicked his cigarette butt out onto the road.

Ray slowed and turned down a dirt road, and in the distance I glimpsed Aunt Bernie's farmhouse. It was just how you'd described it, Mama. Like a place out of time.

The white farmhouse, covered with blistered paint, was tidy. Intricately carved posts ran along the front porch, where a faded green rocker sat, along with a small wicker table. Above the door was a star made of tin with a design punched into it. I remembered that you'd said your daddy made things as a boy at his father's machine shop. Next to the house was a silver silo, an old red barn, and an outbuilding where a rusty tractor sat like a skeleton. Next to the barn was a small pigpen where two hogs lay on their sides, resting in the heat.

When we stopped in front of the farmhouse, Ray's resolve seemed to melt, Mama. He leaned on the steering wheel, his voice tight.

"This is for the best, girl. You gotta know that."

I got out and slammed the truck door. Hard.

Ray got out my suitcase and the Kroger bag. I carried the small box from Littleton Funeral Home.

Aunt Bernie came out onto the porch. The first thing I noticed was how she looked like an older version of you, Mama, except weathered, carved out of stone. Her eyes reminded me of storm clouds, gray and a little threatening. It didn't look like she smiled much. She wore seriousness like a black cloak.

Aunt Bernie opened the screen door for us, letting us in without a word. The porch door led into the kitchen—the cleanest kitchen I've ever seen. It shined in the sun, the gleaming toaster shooting rainbows of light all around us.

Through an arched doorway was the living room, with a fireplace and wood mantel. A nubby brown couch sat in front of the fireplace, draped with a crocheted afghan, just like the one in our trailer. Two stuffed armchairs with lacy sleeves on their arms faced an old television with legs. A wood cabinet with glass doors held a handful of figurines and painted china. Pictures of country landscapes hung higgledy-piggledy, itching to be straightened, and a big painting of the Last Supper took up a whole wall above the television.

It was comfortable—not fancy at all—but boy, Mama, was it spic-and-span. The side tables were shiny with polish, and the throw rug looked like no one had ever set foot on it. It was still and quiet—like a museum—like Aunt Bernie was the sole caretaker of an exhibit where a family had once lived. You could almost imagine a mysterious circumstance somehow made them disappear, and it was her duty to kept it exactly how it had always been. I was afraid to move for fear of touching something and messing it up.

She looked at Ray, her mouth pursed. "Thank you for bringing her. I'll see to her well-being, I can assure you."

Ray's eyes were watery, focused on his feet. He gave me a quick pat on the shoulder. I stood, unmoving, still holding the box.

His eyes flickered my way. "I'll unload your bike."

He asked Aunt Bernie from the doorway, "Okay if I put it in the barn?"

Ray ducked out the screen door, and that was it. I was

47

alone with Aunt Bernie, my only living relative—a woman who clearly didn't know what to do with a twelve-going-on-thirteen-year-old niece who'd appeared suddenly in her kitchen, with a sourpuss face.

I stood rooted to the spot with the little box. My suitcase and the Kroger bag rested at my feet. With all my being, I wanted to run outside to catch Ray before he pulled out of the drive, and scream, *"Don't you dump me here, Ray! Don't you dare. Take me home, right now!"*

Except I don't think either one of us knew where home was anymore, Mama, without you in it.

Aunt Bernie tried to take the Littleton Funeral Home container from my hands. But I wasn't letting go. That little box was all I had of you.

We proceeded to have a tug-of-war over that box, Mama.

"I'll take this now," she said.

I shook my head. I was trying to be polite, but considering the circumstances, I didn't have much choice but to be defiant.

She looked me firmly in the eye. "I'll just put it over here on the mantel. That way you'll know where it is."

I shook my head harder and gripped the box tighter.

"Dulcie, you needn't be stubborn. . . ." She grappled

for words as she pulled the box toward her. "We'll just put it . . ."

It.

Clearly she didn't want to say aloud what we both knew was in there.

She made one final firm tug, and my sweaty palms released it, before she was aware I'd let go.

The box tumbled to the floor.

It landed sideways, the top askew. The small plastic bag inside the box had split and spilled its contents—a dusty trail along the clean wood floor.

Welcome home, Mama, I thought.

Aunt Bernie's face drained of color, her eyes blinking and uncomprehending. Then she flew into action. "Get the broom and dustpan. That closet there."

I wasn't sure if she was frantic because her floor was dirty or because her sister was spewed all over it.

By the time I'd found the broom and dustpan, Aunt Bernie had already gotten a plastic bucket with soapy water and a washrag. While I held the dustpan, she swept up ashes. We upended them into the box. Aunt Bernie wiped up the floor lickety-split, as if the spill hadn't happened at all.

After bringing the box to the mantel, Aunt Bernie

placed it there among some knickknacks, where it looked out of place next to a gaudy vase filled with plastic flowers. She tidied up, then looked at me and said, "Honestly."

Which is just what she said the night I hit Loretta Swinson with the Bible.

Once we'd gotten back inside and were under the kitchen light, she took one look at my ripped dress and scratched legs, then clicked her tongue. "Honestly." She shook her head. "Well, the apple doesn't fall far from the tree, does it?"

If she meant I was more like you than like her, she was right. All the ways you were loose and free, Mama, Aunt Bernie was tied up and closed. In the weeks since I'd arrived, Aunt Bernie had never talked about you. She strictly avoided the subject. It was the one thing we had in common.

I caught Aunt Bernie looking at me now and again as if I were a specter rising up out of the floorboards. One time, while she helped me make my bed, almost so quiet I could barely hear it, she said, "You look so much like your mother. Sometimes I think . . . she's right here . . ." But after that Aunt Bernie just shut right up and went back to making hospital corners.

The night of the Bible thumping, I was ready for her to

send me packing. Aunt Bernie dropped her purse onto the counter while I stood waiting for the axe to fall. She dug around in the icebox and spread food on the table—cold chicken, deviled eggs, pickled beets, and a carton of milk. "Are you hungry?"

I nodded, even though I wasn't. It would have been an insult to refuse. After only a few weeks in Shepherdsville, I'd discovered that Aunt Bernie believed in food almost as much as she believed in the Lord. She baked and chopped and prepared the ingredients for a meal as if cooking were a calling from the Almighty above.

Aunt Bernie didn't say so, but my presence had to be certain relief from her usual meals alone. We ate the cold food. The only conversation taking place was outside between the chirping of the crickets and the trilling of the cicadas.

Afterward, while I washed and put away the dishes, Aunt Bernie sat in the living room and embroidered with a hoop and needle, by a single lamp, glasses perched on the end of her nose. She had taken to heart President Carter's words about saving energy.

Remember how we watched him on TV at the diner that winter, Mama, wearing a cardigan sweater, telling everybody to turn off the lights and turn down the heat?

You laughed and talked back at the set. *"If I turned it down any lower, Jimmy, I'd be a corpse at the morgue."* You didn't joke about all the nights we'd spent in the dark because the power had been cut off.

I was used to the dark. Aunt Bernie kept the house as dim as a cave and wouldn't use electricity unless it was a dire emergency. If J. C. said there was a crisis, then Aunt Bernie was on a mission.

I guessed that was what I was, Mama—a kind of crisis.

She looked up from her work. "Take that dress off. Leave it out on the landing, so I can wash and mend it."

Not a word about me hitting Loretta. I figured she was waiting until morning to call Ray at Shirleen's and have him come get me. A part of me wanted that real bad, but another part didn't—the part that wanted to be closer to you in any way I could.

I climbed the creaky stairs up to your old bedroom, where the peeling walls told the story of a girl who'd run away from home a long time before, her things just as she'd left them.

7

p-a-s-s-a-g-e

passage (n.)

*movement from one place to another; a road
or path; that which happens between persons;
interchange*

Once I'd settled in on that first night at Aunt Bernie's,
under the quilt on your bed, the very one you'd slept
under as a girl, and once I'd looked at the same square of
sky through the curtains, surrounded by the things you'd
once touched, I knew you were there with me.

It was in your room that I felt the divine power of
material things, the precious magic of the objects that connected me to you. Knowing you had walked those floors,
looked out the same window at the elm tree in the front yard
and the field beyond, or sat at the small wooden desk and
thought your thoughts, made me feel like a time traveler.

Everything in that room told your story. The painted dresser with the cracked mirror under the eaves, where you'd stood and fixed your hair, applying forbidden lipstick before opening the window and shimmying down the tree to meet your friends. The milk-glass table lamp next to the bed, where you'd read off-limits books—*To Kill a Mockingbird*, *The Catcher in the Rye*, *Lord of the Flies*—sneaking them in and out of the house wrapped in brown paper, disguised as textbooks. The desk with its paper blotter, where your doodles—arrows and stars mostly—told of homework you'd done there, where tears had been shed at having to give up high school, and where love letters had been written to a boy you never told anybody about—which led you to leave this room with one suitcase, the same suitcase that I brought back here with me.

Above the desk a map of the world decorated the wall, confettied with pushpins. Thumbed and dusty *National Geographic* magazines were still packed into a rickety bookcase near the desk. Each issue had tiny scraps of paper marking articles you'd read—about Bora-Bora, Madagascar, Iceland. For each paper marker, for each place, there was a pushpin on the map. You were a world traveler before you ever left this room, Mama. Long before you packed your suitcase and left Shepherdsville, you imagined and dreamed of going to exotic places.

Only the farthest you ever got was Lilac Court.

My very first night at the farm, I slid open the drawer of your desk. In a caddy of nubby pencils and leaky pens, I found your box of silver pushpins. I took out one more pin and pushed it in where I imagined Paint Creek was.

I shoved your suitcase, crammed with my jeans and T-shirts, under the bed, out of sight from Aunt Bernie's snooping. My first-place spelling bee championship cup found a spot on the desk next to my blue *Webster's New World Dictionary*. On the dresser, I found a place for a Polaroid picture that Ray took of us last summer at the lake. Your arm is draped around me, and each of us is wearing the same smile; a perfect day at Neon Beach that we couldn't know would never come again. The Bible that Aunt Bernie gave me was stationed on the bedside table, next to the lamp, so I could pretend to be reading it whenever she came in to check on me.

From then on, every night after Aunt Bernie headed off to bed, I did our usual routine, Mama. I learned a new word. Committed it to memory. Drilled the meaning.

I'd riffle through the dictionary and pick out a word at random—any word that struck me. I wrote it down in the smiley-face notebook that the doctor at Ross County

Hospital had given to me. Then I tore it out, folded it up into a tiny square, and dropped it into the spelling bee cup—one for each night I'd been at Aunt Bernie's.

By the time I hit Loretta Swinson with my Bible, I'd put in more than thirty words.

At the farm I added one new thing to our routine, Mama. Every night I pulled the suitcase out from under the bed, sprang the locks, and took out the only thing of yours I'd grabbed before Ray took all your clothes to the Salvation Army—your Grateful Dead T-shirt. It still smelled like you—Jergens lotion and Dove soap. I wore it to sleep every night and was determined to never wash it. I hid it in my suitcase so Aunt Bernie wouldn't get it in her head to put it through her old Maytag wringer washing machine.

The night I hit Loretta, after a mostly silent meal with Aunt Bernie, I took off my ripped church dress and left it draped over the staircase railing for her to wash and mend. I put on your T-shirt and closed the suitcase—the very same suitcase you'd helped me pack the night before finals. I crawled into bed, too tired to choose a word from the dictionary. I turned out the light and waited for the same old record in the jukebox of my mind to play over and over, round and round—the memory of our last night together.

You seemed happier than you'd been in a long time, as if you were tucking away your troubles. You hummed, laying out my clothes and packing them for the spelling bee, before you left for your shift at the Starliner. "I'm sorry I can't take you up there, baby. I hope you don't mind riding with Mrs. Whitehouse."

You jiggled change in the pocket of your waitress uniform. "Can't give up Friday night tips."

Pulling knee socks out of the dresser and a pressed white blouse from the closet, you said, "I know you'll do me proud."

You ran your hand down my back and kissed my head.

"Besides, having me there will just be a distraction. You can concentrate better without me pacing at the back of the auditorium."

You folded my blouse and plaid skirt gently, then placed a bulky wool sweater on top. "It might get cold."

I flopped onto the bed. "I'll be fine."

"You will. I know you'll be okay without me." You looked at me with that look. You know the one, Mama. That fierce squint that said, *You are my daughter. Not just anybody. My daughter.*

You closed the suitcase with a firm click and ran your hands over its cracked surface.

"Long time since this old thing has had a place to go. Imagine—spelling finals at the state capitol."

You sat next to me on the bed, holding me so close, squeezing me so hard, I could feel how much you wanted it for me. "One more, and you'll be off to the national spelling bee in Washington, DC."

"Mama, let's just do one thing at a time."

"Then you'll be off to Briarwood Academy. I mailed your application yesterday, smarty. You'll get in and be on your way to achieve everything you dream of."

"Mama, think about what you always tell me. Don't count your chickens."

"Then, you'll graduate from Briarwood—"

"Mama, stop it—"

"And go to Harvard or Yale, one of those places, and then you will travel the world. Paris, London, Spain, wherever you want to go. You'll just have to put me into your suitcase and take me with you."

Then, without warning, a gray cloud descended. You got up from the bed and busied yourself with closing drawers and closet doors.

"Long time ago, I thought I'd travel around the world, go places. I only ever went from Shepherdsville to Paint Creek—never left Ohio."

You patted the suitcase. "This is the only thing I took when I left there."

I knew you hated to talk about it, Mama, but I was curious.

"Mama, didn't you miss them? Your parents? Your sister? After you left, didn't you want to see them?"

You looked away at the floor, face as smooth as lake water, your voice soft. "They're long gone now. Bernie is still there, but time changes things."

"Why don't you ever go see her? Give her a call?"

"Dulcie, some things are best left packed away. No use bringing them out and looking them over."

Without another word you picked up the suitcase and left it by the door.

Now that suitcase was back in Shepherdsville, under your bed, where I slept every night.

I rolled over and closed my eyes, trying not to think about it anymore.

Like you said, Mama, some things are best left packed away—no use taking them out and looking them over.

8

a-t-o-n-e-m-e-n-t

atonement (n.)

satisfaction given for wrongdoing; amends

The next morning I woke to Aunt Bernie calling around, doing a phone tree for my salvation. I
could hear her singsongy voice—the one she puts on for
church—through the metal floor register next to the bed.

"Lavinia, it's Bernice. . . . Yes. . . . Well, I did indeed,
and I have to tell you, Dulcie is mighty ashamed of
herself."

I kicked my feet in protest under the quilt. *Ashamed,
my butt. Only wish I'd done it sooner.*

"She'd like the opportunity to apologize. . . ."

I stared at the ceiling. *I would rather walk on hot coals.*

This call was followed by another to Reverend Love.
"She is a lost lamb, Reverend," she cooed, "I will have her

there for Bible study tomorrow evening. It's the only way to keep her on the righteous path to salvation."

I put the pillow over my head.

Finally, Aunt Bernie called Ray, her voice different now—schoolteacher-like, firmer, scolding.

". . . I hope you plan to drive down here. . . . talk some sense . . . apt to be a juvenile delinquent at this rate . . . embarrassed as all get-out. . . ."

I flung the covers back, ready for what redemption Aunt Bernie had in store.

When I went down for breakfast, my ripped Sunday dress was clean and ready to mend, folded on the sideboard. Aunt Bernie was in her apron, rolling pin in hand, a proclamation ready.

"This morning we are baking a cherry pie. This afternoon we will take it over to the Swinsons." She frowned at my T-shirt. "Don't you have a nightgown?" she asked. It's likely she didn't have an appreciation for the Grateful Dead. "Put on an apron."

I tied on one of the frilly aprons she kept on a hook in the pantry. Aunt Bernie plopped me down on the porch with a bowl of cherries to pit, then roosted next to me in her rocker to mend my dress. She wielded the needle with firm conviction, picking up each stray bit of fabric, joining it with another, tightening and pulling, determined to make the cloth lie smooth.

Aunt Bernie remained just as determined to not let on that she was provoked. She reminded me of a teakettle near to boiling. When her whistle finally blew, she broke a thread with a snap and sputtered, "Why did it have to be the Swinson girl, Dulcie? Of all the folks in the congregation to pummel with the Good Book, you had to choose Lavinia Swinson's daughter!"

She put the dress down with a sigh, laid her head back, and rocked.

And rocked.

And rocked.

The morning settled around us. The sounds of field crickets and an occasional bird filled the silence. I pitted cherries, my hands wet with juice, my fingers stained red.

I wished I had a way of letting Aunt Bernie know that my hitting Loretta was as unexpected as snow in July. I knew that my Bible whopping was apt to make things worse between her and Lavinia Swinson. From what I'd seen, Mama, Mrs. Swinson had it out for Aunt Bernie but good.

Like two hens cornered in a cage, they wanted to peck each other's eyes out. There simply didn't seem to be enough space for the two of them on this patch of earth.

Neither one of them seemed willing to relinquish her position as queen bee at the church.

I'd seen how they riled each other up like slithering snakes. The tiff between them had begun when I'd first arrived in Shepherdsville.

Back when she wouldn't let me out of her sight for fear I'd do something unholy or unbiblical, Aunt Bernie herded me into her car one Thursday afternoon to accompany her to the monthly Ladies' Auxiliary meeting down in the basement of the church.

Let me tell you, Mama, you would have thought it was a Sunday. Everybody was dressed to the nines. A dozen country ladies dressed up in their floral prints, adorned with sparkly brooches fished out of jewelry boxes, reeking of eau de cologne, gathered round a table like poker players, doling out cookies and coffee.

One of the ladies, Mrs. Butler, hair piled up like a beehive with hair spray, had prepared cookies—oatmeal, chocolate chip, and sugar—piled on a tray as high as her hair. There were orange melamine cups filled to the brim with black coffee. Everyone stirred packets of sugar or Sweet'N Low into their cups and sipped in unison like it was a choreographed performance—a ballet where everyone had to maintain the illusion of grace.

I grabbed a couple of cookies and settled in to watch the show.

Aunt Bernie was livelier than she was at the farmhouse, asking after this one or that one's family. She nodded a lot and murmured "Uh-huh," like she was listening real hard, but I could tell she found them all just a bit silly. Aunt Bernie deflected any and all inquires about her sudden guest with another question to the asker. She clearly wasn't going to talk about *it*.

It being me.

There was a lot of what I'd call cordiality in that room, Mama, but there was some sharp intention, something slightly dangerous too, like if you didn't watch out, you'd get a cup of hot coffee poured right into your lap, along with a sweet, "Oh, I am *so* sorry."

It was Mrs. Swinson who called the meeting to order, thwacking her spoon up against her plastic coffee cup with a *rap-a-tap-tap*.

"Ladies, let's get started. I printed up an agenda for this afternoon."

She handed out smeary mimeographed copies that left purple ink on everyone's fingertips as they passed the sheets around.

"First of all, we need to address the issue of flowers for

the chapel in July. Given our budget, we'll have to get creative. Number two, we should discuss getting out a calendar to take meals over to the Taylors, since Noreen's had her baby."

Mrs. Swinson took a big breath in, drawing up her chest, her pearl necklace clicking round her neck.

"Lastly, I know that we aren't in charge of how much the church pays the choir director or who gets hired. That has been taken care of in the past by the pastor of the congregation. Reverend Love has made some decisions recently that I think we should approach him about. He might not be aware of how we have always done things."

There was silence in the room. Hair-sprayed heads looked down at the table, suddenly mighty interested in their cups.

Mrs. Swinson kept going, getting louder and more insistent.

"I think the choir robe allotment money should be looked into. What is being proposed is just not in keeping with the way we like to do things, and I believe we should voice our opinion on this matter. I've prepared a petition sheet for everyone to sign that I will present to Reverend Love on behalf of the Ladies' Auxiliary."

Aunt Bernie set her cup down with a clatter. "Lavinia,

what in the world are you saying? Reverend Love has done a fine job. He's been here less than a year, and everything he does, you find a beef with. It is not for us to get into the business of running the church. Besides, that choir robe allotment should go to fixing the furnace before winter."

Mrs. Swinson squared her shoulders against the force of Aunt Bernie's conviction and glared down the table at her. She brushed some invisible crumbs off the table as she gathered wind in her sails.

"Well, I don't think it's time for a political discussion, Bernice. I am not convinced he has cast a wide enough net. I don't think we should settle for the cleaning lady and handmade garments."

Aunt Bernie sat up straight and grabbed the table edge.

"Why don't you say the real reason why you're against Reverend Love's hiring Evangeline Tucker? Because she was Reverend Moore's cleaning lady? You think you are better than other people. That's what this is about."

Mrs. Swinson spoke so forcefully that she spewed spittle across the table. "I don't know what you are implying, Bernice. I think this church could use a properly trained choir director, that's all—as well as factory-made robes."

"Oh my land, Lavinia. Who cares who makes the robes?"

"You don't have to sign the petition, Bernice."

The other ladies passed it in silence, signing their names with a ballpoint pen, clearly too afraid to open their mouths.

I had no idea why nobody wanted that lady Evangeline Tucker to be the choir director, or why they cared about choir robes, but Aunt Bernie stood up when the petition came round to her, marched it over to Mrs. Swinson, and slapped it down on the table.

"I am not signing it. The rest of you shouldn't let her bully you into going against Reverend Love. He should be given a chance to do his job."

That was the day I understood that Aunt Bernie thought the sun rose and set upon Reverend Love. She wouldn't let anybody say anything against him.

Then Aunt Bernie sat back down in her chair and dug her accounting book out of her bag.

"Now if you all would like to turn your attention to real Ladies' Auxiliary business, we can look at the flower budget for July."

Though Mrs. Swinson was the head of the Ladies' Auxiliary, Aunt Bernie had stolen her thunder. It looked as if Mrs. Swinson was threatening to chew up nails and spit out a barbed-wire fence.

Every Sunday since, those two had given each other a wide berth if one saw the other coming. I knew Aunt Bernie was steaming mad at me, because I'd given Mrs. Swinson another thing to hold a grudge about. I was mighty sorry that my having hit Loretta caused problems for Aunt Bernie, but there wasn't anything to be done about it now.

Suddenly Aunt Bernie halted her rocking, causing the creaking of the chair against the porch boards to stop. She frowned and took the bowl from my lap, resigned to the day ahead. A cloud slanted across the horizon, making the field gray, without depth or shadow. Aunt Bernie's voice was soft.

"Let's make that pie."

In the kitchen I watched while she measured flour and cut up butter. Her hands were sure and quick.

"It's the ice water that binds it." She folded and pressed until she had a creamy ball of dough. She rolled and caressed the dough, then draped it over a pie plate like a blanket.

Aunt Bernie stopped and looked at me, her eyes moist whirlpools.

"You might think because we didn't speak, there was

no love between us. I took care of her while our folks worked the fields. I was twelve years old when your mama was born. I practically raised her myself."

She crimped the edges of the dough. "They wouldn't let her stay here after what happened. I never did know which boy it was. Sixteen years old, and they said she was no daughter of theirs. Not any longer. Your mama packed her suitcase and was made to leave."

Aunt Bernie placed the backs of her hands against the corners of her eyes and then placed the bowl of cherries in front of me. "Put sugar in that. One cup."

I went to the cupboard and found the sugar bin right next to the salt bin. I took it down, brought it to the table—afraid the flow of words would stop and I'd never know what she had to tell.

Aunt Bernie's voice was flat, matter-of-fact.

"Your mama brought you back here after you were born. Our folks refused to see her. She stood at that very screen door with you. Did you know that?"

Oh, Mama.

I shook my head, holding my breath.

"You were the most precious thing I had ever seen."

She handed me the measuring cup. "Your grandparents were wrong, Dulcie. They were old and set in their ways.

At the time, I believed I was to respect that, no matter what they'd done. I was taught to honor my parents in all things."

After wiping her hands on her apron, Aunt Bernie reached up and took down a box of instant tapioca from the cupboard.

"I didn't stand up for your mama. She needed me, and I turned her away. I have to live with that."

She measured out four tablespoons of tapioca and tossed it in with the cherries.

"Don't forget to put the sugar in that."

Her face, usually so hard around the edges, was softer suddenly, erased of something.

Aunt Bernie was letting me know she understood why I'd hit Loretta—that I'd done what she couldn't do. She went back outside to gather up my dress and her sewing basket on the porch—the conversation about you seemed to have worn her out. The screen door murmured shut. The bowl of cherries waited, heavy and full.

Then something came over me, Mama. I thought of Loretta and her smug face. *"What about what Dulcie's mother did? Doesn't a person who does that go straight to hell?"*

I picked up the sugar container and put it back in its place in the cupboard. I took down the matching salt bin

70

from the cupboard instead, then poured and measured the crystals with care.

Exactly one cup.

I dumped it into the cherries and stirred.

Aunt Bernie returned with my mended dress and draped it over a chair. "Pour the cherries into the pie plate, over the dough. I'll make a lattice top from the rest of the dough, and we'll be done."

While the pie baked, Aunt Bernie made us breakfast. Left-over ham and biscuits with gravy. She placed the food in front of our places and met my eyes.

"Let us pray."

Something between us had loosened from its hard places. Talking about you, Mama, had made Aunt Bernie more gentle, her sharpness less defined.

I bowed my head, ready for a long-drawn-out prayer. Aunt Bernie had a whole other voice for talking to heaven.

"Lord, today we ask for forgiveness." Then, instead of her usual "Amen," she picked up her fork and said, "Let's eat."

9

c-o-n-t-r-i-t-i-o-n

contrition (n.)

a feeling of remorse for sins or wrongdoing;
earnest repentance

With her bun tidy and my hair brushed, Aunt Bernie and I got spruced up in church clothes, even though it was only Wednesday. The sun blistered at noon, and the heat clustered in the kitchen. The cherry pie glistened on the cooling rack, ready for the journey to the Swinsons'.

When the pie was cool enough to transport, I sat in Aunt Bernie's Oldsmobile—a giant boat of a car—balancing the tin on my knees as we headed off to Shepherdsville. When we got to the center of town, Aunt Bernie took a left at the light and glided the Olds past the post office, the bus station, Marva's Dress Shop, and the filling station, careful to not upset the concoction on my lap.

Town was mostly deserted in the heat. A few men lingered out in front of the hardware and feed store, toothpicks jutting out of their mouths, with nothing better to do, it seemed, than to watch the cars go by.

Shepherdsville did its usual job of parading as candidate for most boring town on earth, but then the strangest thing occurred, changing the landscape altogether. We passed a girl, a bit older than me, walking on the side of the main road in town. She wore an old army jacket and jeans with ragged bell bottoms that dragged below her scuffed boots. She carried a duffel bag, along with a guitar slung across her back.

Aunt Bernie slowed, then backed up and pulled the Olds right up next to her. Leaning out the window, Aunt Bernie called to the girl, "Can we give you a lift somewhere?"

The girl shook her head, her long brown hair hiding her face. She kept walking, ignoring us as we continued to drive alongside her. Aunt Bernie persisted. "It's no trouble."

"No, thanks."

"I don't mind dropping you someplace. I hate for you to be out here on the road by yourself."

The girl stopped, her pretty face distorted with a look that said *I'd rather die*. She rolled her eyes. Her voice full of twang, she said, "Look, lady, I said I don't need a ride. I'm not going far, and I just want to be left alone."

Aunt Bernie gave up. "Well, all right. Be careful. Don't take rides from strangers."

That girl and I exchanged a look, Mama. Hers was mostly full of pity for me. Aunt Bernie had that effect on people.

The girl harrumphed loudly, then picked up her pace, leaving Aunt Bernie in the dust. I wanted to get out and walk with that girl to wherever she was going. It had to be better than where I was headed.

Aunt Bernie drove on.

"I hope she'll be all right. No place for a girl her age to be wandering the countryside. These young people hitchhiking from the bus station to who knows where. It's not proper."

I got the feeling Aunt Bernie did this often. Tried to pick up strays. I also got the idea that her being a Good Samaritan had more to do with you, Mama, than concern for the hitchhiker's well-being. I wondered if she didn't think of you every time she saw somebody lugging a suitcase by the side of the road.

We passed the First Trust Bank and the Old Mill Tavern, the parking lot full of cars. The houses on the side of town where the Swinsons lived weren't mansions by any means, but they were spacious enough. It was another world from the trailer or the farmhouse, that's for sure. Aunt Bernie, who did taxes for many farm families at tax time every year, had mentioned that the Swinsons had three times more money than most folks in Shepherdsville, and they made no secret of it.

The Swinsons' house gleamed with white paint, bright yellow shutters, and lacy curtains at the windows. The perfectly kept lawn was surrounded by a picket fence covered with climbing roses, like Loretta—pretty, with nasty thorns.

We quietly made our way up the walkway to the door and rang the bell. Chimes sounded inside, followed by the yapping of a small dog. I balanced the pie on my palms. While we waited, I entertained myself with visions of Loretta eating it.

From inside, Loretta's mother trilled, "Pepper, stop it, now."

Mrs. Swinson opened the door in fancy shoes and earrings, her makeup threatening to crack in puzzlement. Loretta stood behind her, her eyes hard little pieces of coal. Mr. Swinson, a thin man with very little hair, wearing a suit and tie, appeared. He was holding a small black poodle.

The entire family looked perplexed. Clearly we were the last people on earth the Swinsons had expected to see on their front porch. We stood there while the planet turned on its axis, crank by crank. An uncomfortable eternity passed before Aunt Bernie said, "Dulcie baked you all a pie. It's cherry."

Mrs. Swinson forced a smile, her lipstick spreading. "Well, isn't that nice?" She looked at Mr. Swinson uncertainly. "We just finished our luncheon. Mr. Swinson is on his way back to the bank." She looked at him with panicky eyes. "But you can stay for a minute, can't you, dear? To visit?"

Mr. Swinson's smile was genuine. He didn't seem to share his wife's and daughter's nature.

"Well, sure, happy to."

Aunt Bernie grabbed the pie and presented it with pride. Mrs. Swinson took it with delicate fingers as if it were a bomb. "Won't you come and visit for a moment in the living room? Loretta will get you a cool glass of lemonade, won't you, Loretta?"

She sent her daughter a look that said, *Make it snappy*.

I followed Aunt Bernie into the house, happy to be out

of the crosshairs of Loretta Swinson's hateful eyes.

Cherry pie or no cherry pie, it was war between Loretta and me.

We entered a room filled with plush furniture and shiny tables glistening with polish. Gold-rimmed paintings hung on the walls. A fancy brass clock sat on the mantel under a glass dome. The rug under our feet was a thick blue shag. Aunt Bernie and I sat on the billowy sofa and sank three inches. I swear, Mama, the room was practically lined with dollar bills.

Mr. and Mrs. Swinson perched on chairs opposite us. Pepper flopped down under Mr. Swinson's feet. We all searched the room for someplace to look, and settled on the floor.

Mr. Swinson cleared his throat.

Mrs. Swinson hovered on the edge of her chair, squeezing her hands in her lap as if she wanted to wring them right off her wrists. She called out, "Loretta?" in a faintly desperate voice. "How's it going with the refreshments out there? Do you need some help?"

Loretta's voice came from somewhere in the back of the house. "No, I'm fine. Be right there." I figured she was probably spitting into our glasses right that minute.

Mrs. Swinson gave us a tight smile. "You'll have to

excuse us. Our colored gal up and quit on us recently, so we are having to fend for ourselves."

Aunt Bernie tilted her head, as if to sympathize. Her voice dripping with pickle juice, she said, "Well, that is a pity."

Mr. Swinson gave a terse laugh. "Lavinia, I think you'll survive." Mrs. Swinson gave her husband a look that could have melted his face right off.

The silence that ensued had layers, and when I thought it couldn't get quieter, it did.

Finally, after what seemed like four centuries, Loretta came in with a tray of tall, multicolored metal cups on an Ohio State Fair tray. She set the tray down in front of us and passed the cups out. When she handed one to me, a little lemonade spilled over the top and landed on my dress.

"Oops. I'm sorry," she trilled.

I wiped my dress with my hand and looked at Aunt Bernie. She gave me a smile similar to the one a nurse might give you before she sticks you with a needle. *This is only going to hurt a little.*

Loretta headed back toward the kitchen with the empty tray—I suspect as an excuse to leave the room. Mrs. Swinson commanded her with a syrupy voice. "Loretta, just put that down and have a seat."

Loretta turned from the door, and put down the tray on a side table. She flounced down onto a velvet hassock across from the sofa, and glared.

Nobody said anything. There was some shifting. The heat rose in the room. Surely these people were rich enough to have an air conditioner. More shifting. My palms were slick with nervous sweat. My heart skip, skip, skipped all the way to my Lou and back in the awkward silence.

I swallowed a big gulp of lemonade, relieved at the coolness of it. Mrs. Swinson's smile quivered with effort.

"Well," she said.

Aunt Bernie flushed an unnatural color. "Lavinia, I appreciate your having us." She tugged at her skirt and regarded me. "Dulcie would like Loretta to know that she is truly sorry for what happened at Bible study." She patted my knee. "Aren't you, Dulcie?"

Loretta snarled, "I don't accept her apology. What she did was plain mean, and I don't care if I ever see her again."

Mr. Swinson ran his hand over his head. "Now, Loretta."

Mrs. Swinson adjusted herself, smoothing the knees of her panty hose. Her voice was as sharp as a razor blade. "Loretta, where are your manners?"

I took another sip of my lemonade and held an ice cube in my mouth, letting the coolness drip down the back of my throat.

Aunt Bernie, as calm as a tomcat, pounced on her prey.

"Lavinia, Dulcie has been through a great ordeal. She's not herself right now." Then she turned her gaze to Loretta. "Surely you can be a little more forgiving, Loretta."

Loretta glared. "I'll accept her apology if she says it herself."

Aunt Bernie sputtered, "You know very well she can't." She appealed to Mrs. Swinson, her voice rising. "And . . . Dulcie was provoked—"

Lavinia Swinson interrupted, no longer genial in any way. "Bernice, Loretta did nothing to warrant a physical attack."

Her eyes bored into mine. "Dulcie, I do think you owe Loretta an apology."

Loretta joined her. "Yeah, why can't you tell me yourself? What's with the big act? You're probably just making it up. I'll bet you could talk if you wanted to. You're only trying to have yourself a big old pity party. Poor Dulcie. Boo-hoo."

Mama, I did it again. I did it before I knew what I was doing.

I spat that ice cube right out at Loretta. It hit her smack in the middle of her chest, then fell to her lap with a plop.

All the air went out of the room in a great whoosh. Loretta was up off the hassock, lurching toward me, her obvious intention to inflict bodily harm. Pepper growled at the sudden commotion.

Mr. Swinson grabbed Loretta by the waist and held her back. "Hey, hey, now."

Aunt Bernie held her arm in front of me like you would if you were coming to a stop sign too fast.

Mrs. Swinson, like the empress of all Shepherdsville, rose. With a haughty voice, as if she were speaking to her lowly subjects, she said, "Enough."

Aunt Bernie opened her mouth to say something, but Mrs. Swinson waved her off.

"I appreciate your stopping by and bringing the pie, Bernice, but I think it's best that you leave now, if you don't mind. For the girls' sake."

Mrs. Swinson motioned to her husband and the dog, signaling for them to heel. "Frank, put Pepper out back." Mr. Swinson, red-faced and befuddled, slunk out of the room without another word.

"Loretta, go to your room. Now."

Loretta mouthed silently, "I . . . am . . . going . . . to . . . get . . . you," before she left the room.

Mrs. Swinson opened the front door and ushered us out.

The door closed behind us with a crisp click. We hurried down the walkway to the car, Aunt Bernie's chin leading the way.

I slid into the car's interior. The seat burned the backs of my legs like hellfire. Aunt Bernie started the car. We sat for a minute looking at the house, stupefied.

The lace curtains in one of the upstairs rooms parted.

Loretta's face appeared.

Ever so slowly she unraveled her middle finger and flipped us the bird, pressing it against the glass.

Aunt Bernie blew air out of her mouth so hard, she could have filled a party balloon in one go. She put the car in reverse and backed out onto the main road.

We drove along for a few minutes before she spoke. "I put the salt bin back into the cupboard for you," she said. "An innocent mistake. Definitely unfortunate, but understandable. Baking takes practice."

10

s-a-l-v-a-t-i-o-n
salvation (n.)
a saving from danger or difficulty; rescue

On Thursday evening Aunt Bernie dropped me off at
Bible study with a warning. "Keep your Bible in your
lap and your hands in prayer, Dulcie. The good Lord is
watching you. Don't disappoint him."

I seriously doubted the big man had his binoculars out,
interested in the goings-on in the basement of Redeemer
Baptist Church. I figured he must have better things to do
with his time—wars, floods, famine, and such—but I gave
her a thumbs-up anyway.

Loretta and the usual crowd hung around outside the
church, waiting for Reverend Love to arrive and open the
door. They congregated on the front steps, a pack of wild
wolves, hungry for a meal.

Before I'd thumped Loretta on the head with my Bible, my penance had been limited to whispers and looks, but now the entire Bible study group was united in their efforts to get a reaction out of me.

Lerman Henckle cried out "Meow" when he saw me. The others wailed along with him, making tortured cat noises.

"Meow."

"Meeee-owwww."

"Here, kitty, kitty."

I turned away and looked at the sky. It was a wispy gray, not the bright blue it had been when I'd seen the swan two days before. I refused to cry, Mama, come the devil on stilts or mighty high water.

Darlene, a girl with squinty eyes and a mean streak of a mouth, yelled, "Dulcie, why don't you say something? Cat got your tongue?"

Everybody howled in unison, like it was even funnier now that they'd said it a few hundred times.

Reverend Love pulled his car into the lot. The field grew quiet and my tormentors became interested in their feet suddenly, intent on taking advantage of Reverend Love's trusting nature. They knew they could get away with heckling me when he wasn't around.

They knew I'd never tell.

Reverend Love got out of his dusty blue station wagon, then walked over to the passenger door and opened it. A murmur of curiosity swept through the group.

A girl emerged wearing a ripped T-shirt, black cut-offs, and army boots. Her long, dark hair was parted down the middle. Her eyes were rimmed round with black eyeliner.

It was the same girl that Aunt Bernie and I had seen walking out on the road the day before. She was a mere hummingbird of a person, slight and wiry, her face wounded and tough in its expression. Her hands were in her pockets, and her head was down as she followed Reverend Love to the doors of the church. When the girl got a look at the scraggly bunch waiting there, she shot them a long look of pure disgust. I wondered what in the world she was doing there at the church of all places.

A clean evening breeze sprang up, lifting our dresses and ruffling our hair as Reverend Love struggled with the lock and keys to the front doors. The girl slunk against the side of the building, bringing with her a small portent of change on the wind.

We filed into the basement meeting room and sat down in the corralled metal chairs waiting for us. Reverend Love pulled out a chair for the new girl, and she plopped into it with a thud. He handed her a Bible, then wheeled the portable blackboard toward us. The fan turned back and forth, blowing hair into his eyes, making him look more disheveled than usual.

Reverend Love erased the words from the last Bible study. He fished a piece of chalk out of his pocket. Scripture flowed from its squeaky tip. The room was unnaturally quiet, save for the sound of cracking gum and the chalk grating on the board.

The girl with the dark hair blew enormous purple gum balloons and snapped them into oblivion with zeal. All eyes were on her, fascinated by her every move. I was deeply relieved, Mama. Her presence was an unexpected gift of sorts. I was no longer the most unusual thing to have come down the pike.

Reverend Love said, "Before we start, I'd like you to welcome Faith." He motioned toward the girl with his chalk.

Jason Burdine guffawed like a doofus. "Oh, no way. Who names their kid 'Faith,' anyway?"

Faith stopped him cold. "My parents, you butt-wipe."

Jason shriveled up like a roly-poly bug. He wasn't used to people fighting back.

I liked this girl already, Mama.

Reverend Love ignored them. "Faith will be staying with Mrs. Love and me for a while. Let's go round and introduce ourselves, please. Starting with you, Loretta."

Following Loretta, names were tossed into the circle—Missy, Lerman, Leann, Matt, Jason, and the rest. Of course, they skipped over me.

"Hey, what about that girl?" Faith pointed a finger at me. I couldn't tell whether or not she remembered me from the road. "She didn't say who she was."

Lerman spoke up, "Oh, she don't talk. She's a mute. Dumb as they come."

Reverend Love spoke sharply, "Enough. Sorry, Faith. This is Dulcie. She is having some trouble with her voice. We expect it will return with the good Lord's help."

Leann made a tiny kitten sound. "Meow."

Jason Burdine leaned close to Faith and put his mouth right up to her ear. "Cat's got her tongue."

Everyone except Faith laughed. She rolled her eyes and sneered, "Jesus, what a bunch of freaks." After looking around the room in disgust, she curled her lip at Reverend Love, and challenged him outright. "What kind of rodeo you rope me into, huh? You're holding me against my will, ya know."

A deep silence followed, while we waited for the earth

to open up and swallow her whole. Reverend Love sucked in air like a drowning man.

"Well, the alternative isn't much better, Faith. You can choose your path. You are free to go if you like. But I like to think it is God's will that you're here."

Faith leaned back in her chair. "Whatever you say, Preacher-man." She pulled a long tendril of purple gum out of her mouth, stretched it taut, and then whipped it round and round until the gum wrapped into a tight little wad on her index finger. Then she shoved the wad back between her teeth.

Reverend Love turned to the board and said nothing further to her. While he droned on, citing scripture and verse, having us follow along with the words of those guys Matthew, Mark, Luke, and John, we all watched Faith's antics.

For some time, she drew an elaborate design on her arm with an ink pen, then moved on to destruction of church property. She neatly ripped a page out of the Bible and folded it into a paper airplane with expert precision. We watched in awe as it whizzed past Reverend Love while he was writing on the board. He continued droning and pretended not to notice.

At the end of the meeting, I retrieved Faith's paper

airplane from under the radiator. Smoothing it free of wrinkles, I examined the wings for damage, and tucked it into my Bible.

Reverend Love noticed me. "Dulcie, I'd like to talk to you before you leave."

The others shuffled out, except for Faith. She leaned against the doorframe, waiting for Reverend Love, arms crossed.

I sat back down and stared at the floor, studying a cracked piece of linoleum, careful not to look in Faith's direction. Reverend Love sat next to me, the gold letters on his Bible glinting in the bright lights.

"Dulcie, I've been praying and thinking about you— about what happened on Tuesday, and I think I have a solution to our problem." I waited, knowing I had little to say about whatever punishment he had in mind.

Faith continued to lean against the doorframe, chewing gum, watching us.

Reverend Love went on. "Bernice and I had hoped this group might be good for you, but I don't think it's the best place for you right now."

My heart rose. A small window of hope opened. I clutched the Bible in my lap, the tip of Faith's paper airplane peeking out.

I wanted to jump and shout hallelujah, to sing and dance around the room. No more taunting or whispers. No more stares or catcalls.

I was free, Mama. No more Bible study.

I smiled, giving him my full approval of the plan. He cleared his throat. "I have an idea of something you might like to do instead of Bible study." He nodded toward Faith. "And, I think Faith might be happier as well."

He called out to her as if he hadn't known all along that she'd been eavesdropping on our conversation.

"Faith, I don't think you'd mind not coming to Bible study. Am I right?"

She rolled her eyes. "You're not just whistling Dixie, Preach."

"Dulcie, I'd like to invite you over to supper tomorrow night with Mrs. Love and me. Faith will be there. I'm sure she'll enjoy some company." The look on Faith's face showed that nothing could be further from the truth. "I'd like you girls to meet someone. I've already talked to your aunt. She'll bring you by my house at five. All right?"

Faith appeared irritated, but then I didn't think she would like anything Reverend Love had to offer.

I nodded. Yes, I would come to dinner and see what he had in mind.

This proposal might be punishment or reward, but some light crept into my darkness. I stood up and floated toward the door. If Reverend Love had wanted me to ride to Jerusalem on a camel, I would have done it to get out of Bible study.

Faith hunched near the basement steps, giving me the stink-eye. For the first time since I'd come to this place, I wasn't the unhappiest person in the room. As I scooched past, I handed her the Bible airplane.

She glared at me, crumpled the plane into a tiny ball, and threw it to the ground.

"We're not friends, okay. So don't go thinking we are."

11

c-o-m-m-u-n-i-o-n

communion (n.)

the act of sharing one's thoughts and emotions;
an intimate relationship with deep understanding

Aunt Bernie's favorite pastime, besides cooking, is back-fence talk. She sure does love her some gossip, Mama. I doubt Jesus approves of her habit of hanging everybody's dirty laundry on the Shepherdsville clothesline—airing the scuttlebutt she hears, as free as you please—but that Friday evening as she drove me out to Reverend Love's house for dinner, I got an earful. Head-high corn glided past the car windows as she revealed the events surrounding the sudden and mysterious appearance of Faith.

"Apparently she's a runaway." Aunt Bernie lowered her voice as if somebody might overhear her. "The sheriff's department turned her over to the county. They couldn't locate her people down in Kentucky." She shook her head in disapproval, the silver strands in her brown hair glinting as she sprinkled tsk-tsks into the air.

"Imagine. That girl broke into the church and was sleeping down in the basement."

As we drove closer to town, we passed the church, standing alone out in the field. I thought of that finger game we used to do, Mama. *Here is the church. Here is the steeple. Open the door, and see all the people.* I loved that special trick you used to do to make the people disappear. Redeemer looked forlorn without cars out front, without people milling in groups fixing to go inside and do their spiritual business.

I searched the sky over the church, hoping to see one of the swans flying over the wooded area beyond the fence. Only a few feathery clouds floated over the trees. Now that I'd been cut loose from Bible study, I didn't know if I might get another chance to visit the swan's nest.

We took a left onto an asphalt road. The wind whistled through our cracked-open windows, ruffling papers and Aunt Bernie's account books in the backseat.

"Of all things, I tell you." Aunt Bernie gripped the steering wheel, leaned forward, and peered through the windshield, looking for her next turn. "Instead of handing her over to the authorities, Reverend Love and his wife took her in." She raised her eyebrows, the scandal of it pulling them into hard arches.

"Imagine that." Aunt Bernie clucked her tongue. "Seems dangerous to me, letting an unknown girl, a total stranger, in your house like that." She looked at me, then caught herself. "Well, it isn't as if the girl is a relative or anything of that nature."

Aunt Bernie drove slower than a turtle in a hurry, the story consuming her attention. "That girl would have ended up in the juvenile detention home otherwise. Only the good Lord knows what would have come of her there." She blew out a heavy breath, the thought of it weighing on her. Aunt Bernie sure is afraid of the devil snatching souls, Mama.

"Well, Reverend Love is a decent man, is all I can say—what with his wife expecting a baby and his church obligations—to help that girl in her time of need."

I tried to imagine sleeping in that creepy old basement, with no light. No wonder Faith was irritable.

Reverend Love's wife greeted me at the door. She waved to Aunt Bernie from the porch. Aunt Bernie fluttered her fingers good-bye and drove away, the dust flying from the Oldsmobile's wheels like it was pure relief to drop me off at a preacher's house and have a night off from seeing to my eternal salvation all by herself.

I knew Mrs. Love from church. She was always free with her deep-dimpled smiles, shaking hands, and greeting folks on Sundays. She appeared to have a big ole watermelon under her billowy blouse, fixing to burst.

"So happy you could come tonight, Dulcie. My husband will be right back." She took my hand and led me into the house. "He's gone off to pick up our other supper guest. You'll find Faith out on the back porch."

I figured I'd find out soon enough who it was that Reverend Love wanted me to meet, so I looked around, curious. I'd never been in a preacher's house before, so I wasn't sure what to expect. I thought it would have lots of Jesus pictures and crosses, but the Loves' house looked like any regular folks' house, with a dining table set for a meal. I could see through an open door down the hall that a baby crib was set up.

"You go on back and visit Faith. I'll bring out some lemonade." Mrs. Love opened up a door past the kitchen and pointed the way.

Faith sat on the edge of the porch, a blade of grass between her thumbs, making a fluttery whistling sound by blowing into her cupped hands.

She looked me up and down. "Look what the cat dragged in." She went back to what she was doing, pretending I wasn't there.

I sat down, but not too close. The Loves' tiny backyard bordered on a cornfield with buttery tassels waving hello in the late afternoon air. A fly dive-bombed past my ear. I brushed it away, but it kept coming at me. The sounds of Mrs. Love clinking things in the kitchen floated out the window to us. Next to the house a monarch butterfly landed here and there among the flowers, slowly beating his wings.

I avoided looking in Faith's direction, like you'd do if you came upon a wild animal in the woods. The only safe way to be near was to act unconcerned, else you'd be attacked.

Without warning Faith scooted closer. "I'm not staying long, you know. Soon as I get me some money, I'm gone. That's why I said what I said—about us not being friends." She inspected me more closely to see if I followed her gist, perhaps thinking I had a mental defect as well as no voice. "I'm going to make my way to Nashville. I can sing pretty good. I know a bunch of songs."

That explained the beat-up guitar I'd seen her carrying.

But it didn't explain how she planned on financing her trip. I hadn't seen any money trees dripping with dollar bills in Shepherdsville.

"I'll stay here until the county forgets about me. Sleep on a soft bed for a while, eat some decent food. Let the reverend do his trying-to-save-my-soul thing." She talked like she was convincing herself, all tough on the outside, but her eyes betrayed her. A heap of sorrow shone out from inside her, as strong as a flashlight beam.

I pointed to her skirt—a cotton floral print with daisies and green swirly vines. Definitely not something Faith might have picked out for herself. Same as me. I pointed at my dress with the blue polka dots and yellow stripes.

"Preacher's wife went through the church donations and brought me what she called 'more appropriate' clothing. Pretty ugly, huh?"

I gave her a thumbs-down, and she laughed. "Guess you didn't choose that git-up either?" She pinched her nose together. "Pee-yew." I pointed my finger down my open mouth like I wanted to upchuck.

A door opened between us—things said and unsaid passed through. I wanted to ask her a million questions but had to settle for what she offered freely. Since I'd lost my voice, I'd learned something, Mama. When you are quiet, people tell you more about themselves than they do if you're chattering away.

Mrs. Love brought out two tall glasses of pale lemonade with a bit of green floating on the top. "I hope you don't mind the mint. That's the way we do it in Kentucky, isn't it?" She winked at Faith, as if being from Kentucky was a special club that only they understood.

After she left, we sat swinging our legs off the porch, holding our cool glasses. Faith turned toward me and brought her voice down low, not wanting Mrs. Love to overhear.

"Can you really not talk?"

I nodded.

"Really? You're not trying to psych them out or anything?"

I shook my head.

"Promise?"

I crossed-my-heart-hoped-to-die promised her that I couldn't.

"Weird."

Reverend Love pushed open the screen door and came out onto the porch, wearing light pants and a short-sleeved shirt. He didn't look the same without his church garb. He looked downright ordinary.

"Glad you two are getting acquainted. Come on inside. I want y'all to meet someone."

We followed Reverend Love to the small living room tucked into the front part of the house. Mrs. Love was just setting out some lemonade on the coffee table by their guest—the woman with the halo of silver-gray hair that I'd seen singing at the front of the choir, on the same day I saw the swan.

"Ladies, may I introduce you to Miss Evangeline Tucker."

I realized right away, Mama, that this was the famous Evangeline Tucker that had the Ladies' Auxiliary in such commotion. Miss Tucker was older than I'd first imagined, yet her face glowed with light, her dark eyes like liquid stars.

"Miss Tucker is our new choir director at Redeemer. She's just returned from visiting her sister down in Atlanta. Evangeline, these are the two girls I mentioned to you. This here is Faith, and this is Dulcie."

Miss Evangeline Tucker didn't say a word. A smile danced on her face. Her manner was as straight as an arrow, determined to get under all the pleasantries, aiming straight at my heart. She took my hand and held it. I felt a warmth coming from her, as if someone had draped a blanket around my shoulders.

Faith—who, I was quickly learning, said whatever popped into her head—sputtered, "Preach told me you could help me with my music, but he didn't say nothing about you being colored." She stared at Miss Tucker, inspecting her closely.

Evangeline Tucker leaned into Faith and grasped her hand as well. "I am many things, honey. Colored is only one of them. Does it matter to you?"

"No. Preach just didn't mention it, is all."

"Well, now. Reverend didn't mention that you were a pistol either, so we'll have to make do as we are."

Faith shook Miss Tucker's hand firmly. "Good by me. Glad to meet you."

Reverend Love filled us in. "Miss Tucker is a valuable member of our congregation, as she is our new choir director—our own musical muse. She'll choose the hymns for services each week, lead the singing of them, and take care of a thousand other things that I can't keep my finger on."

He put his hand on my shoulder. "Evangeline, sometime you'll have to tell Dulcie the story of how you came to Shepherdsville—about the swan leading you to the church."

I got goose bumps again, Mama.

The memory of the swan flying above the church rose in my mind again: the little clearing in the woods, as perfect as a picture, was waiting for me.

Almost as if he read my thoughts, Reverend Love said, "We were swan-watching the other night, Dulcie and me. But we weren't lucky enough to see one, were we, Dulcie?"

I shook my head, keeping my secret. Evangeline gazed at me, like I was a crystal ball she was peering into. "Finding a swan's nest, that's a sure sign of blessedness. But to see a swan in flight, that's nature's way of showing you a path, a compass for your soul."

Some people radiate mysteries and deep secrets, Mama, and Evangeline Tucker was one of them. I was eager to hear what she had to tell.

"Well, now. Come sit beside me for a bit."

Faith and I settled into the sofa on either side of her.

Reverend Love took a seat, and the adults talked about this and that: the weather, the congregation at church, money needed to fix the furnace, and the coming baby.

Occasionally Miss Tucker would rest her hand on my knee or pat my hand as if to say, *You still with me?* I swear, Mama, she could say things without really saying them.

Mrs. Love, or Mary, as we were to call her, announced dinner, and we went in to the table. Miss Tucker didn't move like an older lady at all. She was graceful, floating lightly on her feet. I was placed on one side of her, and Faith on the other. Mary brought out roast beef, potatoes, and green beans. Everyone passed and poured and drank and ate, and still no word about what Reverend Love had in mind or why we were to meet Miss Tucker.

During dessert—Bisquick shortcakes with strawberries and cream—Reverend Love said, "Miss Tucker needs some assistance at the church tomorrow morning. She has some things she could use some help with, and I believe you two are just the ticket."

Miss Tucker spread a smile onto her face like butter, her eyes warm.

"But you'll call me Evangeline, won't you?"

After dinner we settled in the living room, and the adults had coffee. Evangeline leaned back in a soft armchair. "Faith, Reverend Love said you're a singer and a guitar player too. Why don't you play us a little something?"

The Loves encouraged her to play for Evangeline. I was surprised that Faith agreed so easily, but she went and got her banged-up instrument. The strap lay tattered on her shoulder as she tuned and fiddled with the strings.

It occurred to me then, Mama, that that old piece of wood might be the nearest thing to a relative she had.

"Um, this song is my favorite. I remember my mother used to sing it to me, when I was little, before she run off."

Faith's voice, pure and sweet, revealed an inside that didn't at all match the outside she showed the world. The melody of her song transformed the room, making it sparkle somehow.

> *Down in the valley,*
> *Valley so low;*
> *Hang your head over,*
> *Hear the wind blow.*

After Faith sang, Evangeline led Faith and me outside to "take in the night air," she called it. The three of us stood in the Loves' front yard as the darkness of the coming night layered the fields with deeper hues, swirling, impending stardust here and there. June beetles started up their music, and lightning bugs flickered all around us. An occasional mosquito buzzed past, but refrained from landing, giving us respite from having to slap them away.

Evangeline took our hands and whispered, "Magic hour."

The first star appeared, a tiny pinprick of light above us. Faith and Evangeline and I stood underneath it, aligned in a constellation of our own making, while the great world spun and whispered secrets to us.

12

q-u-i-e-s-c-e-n-t
quiescent (adj.)
quiet; still; inactive

The next morning, after breakfast, I hurried through my chores, fed slop to Aunt Bernie's two hogs she was fattening up for fall, and headed for the barn. I dug my old bike, Maybelle, out from where Ray had left her. The smell of long-gone animals and musty hay bales caused me to pinch my nose when I opened the door. A long rope with a big knot on the end hung down from the rafters. I touched it—surely something you'd once enjoyed, Mama. I pictured you swinging, wild and free, happy to escape farm chores and endless Bible reading.

Ray had left my bike leaning against a dilapidated feed trough. I wheeled Maybelle outside to see if she was in rideable condition. She definitely needed sprucing up for the trip to church. I'd promised Evangeline that I would meet her and Faith at Redeemer that morning.

Time was wasting, and I wanted to head out right away. I wondered what big mystery Evangeline had in store. But mostly I wanted to see if the swans behind the church were still there. Maybe they had been a trick of the light or a figment of my imagination. I figured if I beat everyone to church, I could retrace my steps over the fence and see if the swans were truly as real as my memory of them.

In the house, Aunt Bernie was baking up a feast for Sunday afternoon potluck the next day, glad to be rid of me and my ineptness in the kitchen. She made me a ham sandwich and shooed me out of her way.

Aunt Bernie planned to spend that afternoon at WGOD, so I was off the hook from having to keep her company. She'd proudly told me once that WGOD broadcast as far as seventy-five miles away from its tiny tower in Shepherdsville. Her pencils and account books were lined up next to the back door, ready for her job managing the donations that came into the station.

Her transistor radio on the counter blared out hymns, and Aunt Bernie sang along. She can't carry a tune to save her soul, Mama. Aunt Bernie maintained that WGOD was using the radio to broadcast the Bible's good word. To my mind, all that gospel music turned up so loudly could only lead to loss of hearing.

I searched under the sink and came up with S.O.S pads and some paper towels. After some scrubbing and a spray of the garden hose, Maybelle was somewhat less of a sorry sight.

Aunt Bernie had fashioned a bag for me out of old dress cloth so that I could carry my Bible when I went to church. I took the Bible out and replaced it with my notebook and some pencils. I tucked the bag and the ham sandwich into the crooked basket on Maybelle, and took off.

The morning sun beamed hot enough for tar bubbles on the road to puff up, ready to pop. They snapped and crackled under Maybelle's wheels as I rode.

Back at the house, I'd sneaked a pair of shorts on under my dress. Once I was out of sight of the kitchen windows, I pulled up my skirt and tied it around my waist in a knot, leaving my legs free to pump the pedals. If she'd seen me, Aunt Bernie would have had a load of kittens.

When I'd gained enough speed, I coasted, my arms straight out like a bird aiming to take flight. I was breathless when I pulled into the church parking lot—exhilarated, like I'd just gotten off the Ferris wheel at the Paint Creek county fair. I was happy to be out from under Aunt Bernie's thumb at last.

The church lot was empty, the building deserted. I wheeled Maybelle to the side of the church and leaned her up against the wall.

The long grass in the field snapped at my ankles as I ran toward the fence. I hopped over and quickly made my way into the thicket. Sunlight peeked through the trees, dappling the ground with spots of gold. Tiny wildflowers, white and purple, led the way. The woods and the narrow clearing shimmered in the daylight. When I reached the pond, not a creature was in sight.

I waited, disappointment rising. Maybe I *had* imagined seeing those swans that night. Maybe I *was* as cracked as a walnut, like they said—seeing things. There were no swans now—only sedge grass and cinnamon-colored cattails waving at me. The nest was empty.

I was certain the swans had vanished or were just a vision I'd conjured up out of the darkness, and my heart threatened to crack.

They were gone—like you, Mama, like Lilac Court, like my voice.

I sat on the gnarled tree limb near the weeping willow,

grateful to have this place all to myself, where I could talk to you. I knew you could hear me, Mama, even if I couldn't say the words out loud.

I closed my eyes, and everything came back. The state spelling bee finals. The moment when everything changed.

The word was "metamorphosis." *Webster's* definition: "a transformation; a change of condition, appearance, or function."

Standing at the microphone in the auditorium in Columbus, with my eyes closed, the word assembled in my head. The letters appeared like writing on the blank slate of my mind, and the taste of them formed in my mouth. I took a breath and exhaled, ready to speak.

At that moment I saw Ray standing at the back of the auditorium. The stage lights were bright, and I couldn't quite make out the expression on his face, but something in the way he held his body sent a thunderbolt through me as if we were connected by an electric current.

Instantly I understood that you were gone. My mouth was still in the process of forming words, when the caller spoke. "Miss Dixon, I'll repeat the word. The word is 'metamorphosis.'"

My lips met again and again, but the sound that came

out of me was the sound of someone muzzled, mouth stuffed with cotton.

"Mmmm . . . mmm."

Unaware of the trouble I was in, the caller gave the time warning. I continued trying to make sound, but nothing came out.

I don't remember how I got from the stage to the car. I don't remember any of the words Ray spoke. I felt cold—I remember that—my limbs numb, my teeth hitting together. I recall not being able to stop shaking. Ray took off his coat and draped it over me. The vibration of Shirleen's car made a sound, a murmur that hummed, *Mama-mama-mama-mama*, over and over, until it put me to sleep.

I woke up in my own bed, and for a second it was just an ordinary morning. Until everything came back in one great wave.

You were gone, Mama.

The very fact carved out a piece of me, made me hollow.

Empty. Nothing inside.

I didn't even have enough energy to cry, Mama. I lay in my bed and watched the shadows on the wall. Until the shadows became people—Ray, Shirleen, neighbors.

Darkness came in and out, like the tide. I just wanted to go under that tide and stay under. Stop breathing and have it be done. But no matter my thoughts, the waves came, one after the other, my breath going in and out. The earth kept spinning, but I wasn't part of it.

That's when Ray took me to the mental ward and left me—where they told him my voice would return with time—where they gave me the smiley-face notebook to write down my thoughts. That was when Ray decided he couldn't be a daddy to me, and decided to dump me in Shepherdsville with Aunt Bernie—where the only person I could talk to was you. Everything led back to that day, Mama, like a heavy chain I wore, each link connected to the next, long and heavy enough to drag me back down to that dark place.

Something out of the corner of my eye brought me back to the pond. I sat up, startled, nearly falling off the branch. I grabbed the tree bark, rough under my fingers. My heart lifted, Mama.

Perhaps they had been on the other side, feeding or napping in the tall grass, but suddenly, without a sound, the swans appeared, their babies following behind them. They glided into the middle of the pond, a beautiful and silent parade, just for me.

13

v-e-s-t-m-e-n-t

vestment (n.)

a robe; gown; garment worn by officiants or choir members during certain services

I found Evangeline in the long, narrow room off the sanctuary—the vestry, she called it. She'd decorated every nook and cranny of it with colorful trinkets. Bits of glass dangled on strings in the windows, casting prisms of shiny rainbows. Knitted bits of yarn, ripped quilts, and pieces of cloth were braided into rugs on the floor. The tottery old shelves were loaded with treasure, bits of nature tucked here and there: dried berries, blue bottles full of flowers, glittery rocks, and tree branches arranged in the corners.

Tendrils of smoke twirled from a stick of incense that made the room smell like honey and wild things.

Above a rusty sink an old advertisement signboard had been turned around to the wall. On the back were painted words in a child's writing: "Every good and perfect thing is from above."

Evangeline stood in front of an ironing board, pressing a long ribbon of purple fabric. A cup of coffee, the smell earthy, sat steaming nearby. She hummed to herself, incense smoke curling above her head. When she heard me come in, her face crinkled, her eyes shiny. She took my arm and led me farther into the room. "Welcome, welcome, come on in. Look around. Make yourself at home."

She waved her arm, an invitation to survey her kingdom while she returned to her ironing. I set my bag down on a table, fascinated with the odds and ends scattered around the room.

A chipped wardrobe stuffed with tattered gold choir robes took up most of one wall. A box was open beside it on the floor. Hanging on a hook, on the back of the door that led to the sanctuary, was Reverend Love's church garb with the special scarf he wore around his neck on Sundays. A wringer washing machine stood in the corner, and several long banquet tables were opened across the room from side to side. Bright lengths of fabric ran the distance of the tables, rainbow colors spread out every which way.

On top of the cloth, white paper simplicity patterns were laid out, the sleeves glinting with silver pins, like angels with sparkly wings.

Evangeline sprinkled water onto the fabric she was pressing. "Out with the old, and in with the new."

I screwed up my face. I had no idea what she was talking about.

She beamed and pointed to the shiny material. "Choir robes."

I touched one of the patterns. It crinkled under my fingers. I gathered that this was what Mrs. Swinson and the others were up in arms about.

"We're going to make us some new ones. I shopped all the colors I could find at the Bolt and Spool. Mr. Purcell let me have the discontinued cloth in exchange for sewing up some sample dresses for their display window." She stopped. "Do you know how to sew, child?"

I shook my head.

"Well, I aim to teach you. You'll be able to whipstitch come sundown."

She pointed to the wardrobe. "First thing we're going to do is pack up these old robes. Been here since I don't know when." She propped up her iron and pulled its plug from the wall. "Take those off their hangers, fold 'em, and put 'em in that box. They'll make good quilt squares for the sewing circle, come fall."

Evangeline spread out bolts of fabric while I did as she'd asked. I pulled choir robes down from their hangers and arranged them carefully in the box. They were frayed, the gold faded, the fabric shiny with wear in places. Each robe had a yellowed tag sewn inside the collar, names written and crossed out in faded laundry marker—choir members who'd worn them long Sundays ago.

Evangeline looked at her watch. "Now, where do you suppose Faith got up to?"

I shrugged my shoulders. Maybe she'd taken off to Nashville.

Evangeline narrowed her eyes, looking into the distance as if she could see something I couldn't. "Faith is a wandering spirit. That gal has yet to find her true home, so she can't help but seek to find one."

We worked in silence for a bit. Me folding, her ironing, the morning dust motes floating around us.

Then, I found *your* robe, Mama. The second to last one in the wardrobe—your name written on the collar, faint ink still there after so many years. *Emma Dean Dixon.*

I sat down hard on the floor. *Oh, Mama. Mama. Mama.*

I hugged that robe, wrapping myself in it, letting its

softness caress me. I don't know how long it was while I tried to smell you, feel your arms around me, imagine you there beside me.

Evangeline stood behind me and helped me up, slowly unraveling me from the robe.

She looked at the collar for a long time, as if it were telling her a story. "This robe was your mama's?"

I closed my eyes, my throat closed so tight, I could barely breathe. When I opened my eyes, she'd hung your robe back in the wardrobe. "That's yours, honey. It will be here when you want it. You need comfort where you can find it."

Evangeline brought me a cup of water and sat me down in the chair in front of her. She waited with me, the quiet surrounding us. She didn't coddle me, just held my hand under hers and talked to me in her low, rich voice.

"Sometimes you might feel like you are drowning in a deep, dark pool. Loss might threaten to grab you and sink you. What we feel for those we lost is still love. Love isn't all pretty feelings and promises of no heartache. But love is what you have to grab ahold of and use to pull yourself up and out of it, as best you can. The love is what you hang on to, hear?"

Evangeline knew the language of heartache, Mama, and she was teaching it to me.

She patted my arm. "Understand?"

I did my best to smile.

"Now grab those pins and follow me." I picked up a pincushion shaped like a strawberry. Evangeline positioned pins in her mouth and then pulled them out one by one as she attached the patterns to the cloth spread out on the table in front of her. She moved quickly, pushing each pin in and another behind it, following along the blue line at the edge of the pattern.

"See?"

I nodded, doing my best to follow along with her.

"That's good." She watched me for a minute, humming under her breath.

Then Evangeline said the strangest thing, Mama.

"I expect you did some visiting this morning, judging from the state of your shoes." Evangeline smiled and kept pinning robes.

I looked down, and sure enough, my Keds were tinged green from the field and were wet at the toes.

From a large basket Evangeline brought out scissors, then cut along the edge of one of the patterns, all neat and crisp. Her fingers were long and delicate, the nails short.

"Now, since you're curious, I'll tell you what you need to know. There are mute swans, and then, there are trumpeters who honk as loud as a truck horn." Evangeline bent over the fabric, talking while she worked. "The mute ones are the kind that nest in this part of the country." She handed me pattern scraps, gesturing for me to drop them into an old ice cream bucket under the table. "But you best be careful if you happen upon swans. You don't want to get too close to their nest."

She pointed the scissors at me. "They're mighty fierce if riled up. They can take a man down if he threatens them. Uh-huh, I've seen it, you best believe."

Evangeline looked over to check her pinning. "Swans are protective of their young ones. They'll fight to the death if they have to."

She smoothed out fabric and cut patterns as she talked, her voice silky. "They do love a little corn muffin or a bit of greens. A moist crust of Wonder Bread. Not too much though. Just a little, now and again." She handed me a pair of scissors.

"Here. Ready to cut. Just follow along the edge."

Evangeline guided my hand with hers, leaning next to me, her breath warm with the scent of apricots and coffee. "There you go."

She watched me for a moment, then pulled paper scraps out of the ice cream bucket. Using her scissors, Evangeline snipped delicate edges and rounded corners, her fingers nimble and quick—transforming the paper into the shape of a swan. She placed it flat against the windowpane. The sunlight glowed like gold through it.

"The female swan is called a pen, and the male is a cob." She cut out another paper swan, followed by tinier ones. "The babies are cygnets." Evangeline seemed to understand what I wanted to know about the swans as she unraveled their mysteries to me. She told me how to communicate to them and how to signal with my body that I meant them no harm.

"Swans are apt to mate for life and are the most faithful of God's creatures. They're smart, too. They remember human faces and know who has been kind to them, and who hasn't."

It was clear that Evangeline, like Reverend Love, knew about the swan nest out behind the church. Knowing she might have been to my secret place made me feel closer to her. Evangeline commenced with humming again, the melody light, a good accompaniment for the task.

By the time Faith finally arrived, we'd already cut out five robes in different colors.

Reverend Love poked his head in the door.

"My apologies, Evangeline. We were running late this morning. Mary didn't feel up to making breakfast. The baby kicked up a fuss all night and kept her awake. Getting ready to make an appearance, I expect." He yawned. "I'm not much at pancake-making. I burned a few, didn't I, Faith?"

From the look on Faith's face, I gathered more had gone on than pancake-making—more like clothes-changing and face-scrubbing. She wore an ugly cast-off dress, obviously another from the church giveaways. Without her eyeliner, she appeared to be a different person altogether—less defensive, less definite. Tender, somehow.

Reverend Love raised one brow as he surveyed the bolts of fabric laid out before him.

"Evangeline, those robes are going to be something, all right. I appreciate you going to all this trouble."

Evangeline harrumphed. "No trouble at all." She pointed to Faith and me. "I've been blessed with some mighty fine helpers. Anyhow, now the ladies of the church got no reason they can't put that new robe money toward fixing the furnace. No sense you working, come wintertime, with your overcoat and gloves on."

Reverend Love considered this. "I think it's a better

use of our budget. I appreciate you finding a way to get us the fabric without spending a penny of church money. Come wintertime, we'll be grateful for it, and we'll have new robes, too."

Evangeline indicated the old garments we'd folded into the box. "Well, hand to God, these poor robes are moth-eaten and threadbare, not fit to sing hallelujah. These gals can sew up new ones in no time."

Reverend Love tilted his head, not trying to hide his smile. "I'll be upstairs in my office if you need anything."

He gave Faith a little push. "Go on now." She frumped into the room, with a sour face.

Evangeline put an arm around Faith and tucked her in under her wing like a duckling. "I just about gave up on you. Thought we'd lost you already."

Faith allowed Evangeline to guide her over to a table, next to me.

"Wouldn't want to miss out on the fun." Faith smirked and sat down with a plop.

"Dulcie will show you how to pin and cut the fabric."

Faith reluctantly took the scissors and pins, her face a scowl. "What's all this for anyway? Looks like a circus rode into town and left the tent."

"You ever hear of the robe of many colors?"

Evangeline asked. Faith shook her head.

"Back in Bible days, folks all wore the same dull robes. Until one day, a favorite child named Joseph was given a robe of many colors by his father to show honor. These colors will speak out and show that we are all God's favorite children. With your help, I aim to have new choir robes ready for Baptism Sunday in a couple of weeks."

"Baptism Sunday?"

"The day we start as fresh as a newborn baby. As clean as a whistle."

Faith looked positively horrified. "Sorry. I'll miss it. I'll be long gone by then."

Evangeline smiled, something hidden in the spread of her lips. "You reckon so?"

Faith leaned back in her chair. "I know so."

Evangeline put her hand on Faith's shoulder. "All we're going to worry about right now is pinning and cutting. When we use our hands for good, the world falls away."

Faith shook her head, not buying what Evangeline was selling.

After a few attempts at following along the pattern, Faith accidentally jabbed herself with a pin and yelped. She mouthed a word you wouldn't find in the Bible and stuck her finger into her mouth, then sucked on the pinprick of blood. Evangeline retrieved the pincushion from the floor where Faith had dropped it and set it down beside Faith. "Breathe. Slow down. We're in no hurry."

Evangeline returned to snipping fabric, the sound of her humming and the swish of her scissors whistling an accompanying rhythm.

Then she said to nobody in particular, "No use running from things, anyhow. You just bring them troubles right along with you wherever you go. They get mighty heavy, those troubles. Sometimes you just have to set 'em down."

14 ❧

v-e-n-g-e-a-n-c-e

vengeance (n.)

the return of an injury for an injury

The sun hit me full in the eyes when Aunt Bernie swept the curtains open in my room the next morning. Her particular Sunday fury was a mission of utmost importance—to get to church early before everybody else. She wanted to make sure that the flowers were positioned on the altar and the after-church coffee was brewing in its pot.

She also liked to beat everybody else there so that the casseroles, Jell-O, and cookies that came into the basement kitchen would be arranged on the tables and placed in the icebox as she wished them to be. It made her happy to oversee each and every aspect of the social hour that followed church services. She fulfilled these obligations,

Mama, as if it were her rightful place, her God-given duty, like the queen of England's job.

I bumped into Mrs. Swinson and Loretta prancing into church, carrying a fancy cream concoction in a pie tin. Mrs. Swinson shot me a wicked-stepmother smile. The red lipstick from her lips stuck on her teeth, making her look like someone who ate children for breakfast.

"Well, if it isn't Dulcie Dixon. Thank you ever so much for your cherry pie. Unfortunately, our little dog, Pepper, got at it and we had to throw it away. I'm sure"— she patted my arm—"it was delicious."

Loretta guffawed. "Poor thing puked all night."

Mrs. Swinson laughed. "Oh, honey, that's what happens when you eat out of the trash."

She thrust out her cream-topped monstrosity. "If you would be so kind as to take this down for us. We don't want to miss the beginning of services." They sashayed away, their tails wagging.

By the time I'd finished helping Aunt Bernie arrange foil-wrapped plates and casseroles, we barely had enough time to find seats in the sanctuary.

Aunt Bernie handed me a church bulletin with a picture of Redeemer Baptist on the front, its giant white cross even more outsize than the one in real life. I was happy to see that Reverend Love's sermon was on a subject near and dear to my heart.

Redeemer Baptist Church

Sunday, July 10, 1977

Pastor—Zachariah Love

Choir Director—Evangeline Tucker

Sermon: Does Church Have to Be Boring?

Soon enough most of the church bulletins became fans in the heat; the entire congregation transformed into an undulating sea of white paper waves. Evangeline was up at the altar, her arms waving in flight, palms up to the heavens, leading the choir—those few souls who'd decided to show, despite the heat and any misgivings about her. As the new choir robes weren't ready yet, only perspiration decorated the choir's Sunday best. The organ downright drowned them out, shaking the windowpanes.

> *For the beauty of the earth,*
> *For the beauty of the skies,*
> *For the love which from our birth*
> *Over and around us lies.*

Aunt Bernie sang out of tune next to me, as loud as a trumpet. I mouthed the words, imagining my voice drowning hers out. When the hymn ended, she looked in the Swinsons' direction, and whispered, "People seem to be boycotting choir this morning."

It did seem like a few folks were missing from the choir; in particular, the Swinsons. I hoped Aunt Bernie wasn't fixing to join up, because that would have required earplugs for the whole congregation.

Reverend Love leaned into the pulpit, issuing forth words of good and evil, salvation and righteousness, but if he got to the heart of the matter, I never did know, for my mind had since left the building.

Mama, I don't know what happens to time in church, but everything slows down. Each second becomes a year, and each minute becomes an eternity. Church is a perfect haven for daydreamers and doodlers, and I took advantage of it.

I took one of the little pencils out from the back of the pew in front of us, and on the cover of the church bulletin, I sketched a lone swan in flight next to the cross, wings outstretched, its long neck reaching toward the heavens, soaring into my daydreams.

The little pond beyond the church beckoned me. The

swans, their elegant bodies sliding through the water, called me to worship their beauty. I ached to go to them and leave the confines of this human sea of starched shirts and perfumed smiles.

When the service ended, I wandered down to the basement, making my way to the long banquet table set out with food. I filled my pockets with corn muffins, then sneaked out to the parking lot with a cup of fruit punch.

Poor old Marlow sat chained to the door handle of the Burdine's truck, his tongue extended, panting in the sunshine. I put the punch cup down in front of him, and he gladly lapped up the contents, slurping with pleasure. Coat dirty, nose warm, he let me pat the top of his head, then flopped back down in the dirty gravel, seeking shade under the truck.

Loretta and her girl-gaggle came out of the church. Jason, Matt, and the other boys followed behind. They were balancing cups and plates piled with food in their hands as they made their way to the picnic tables—away from the basement and the eyes of their parents.

I made sure they didn't see me as I sneaked around the other side of the building.

I hurried through the field, clutching my Bible bag,

the muffins wrapped in a napkin inside. At the broken fence I climbed over and into the clearing, to the place where the swans nested.

It seemed a world away, Mama.

Just beyond the bank the swans floated, gliding with ease through the brackish water. I ventured a bit closer. The one I presumed to be the male, because of his size, I knighted with the name Mr. Cobb. He raised his wings as if to warn me not to come any closer. His snow-white feathers caught the sunlight, his beak appearing hard and dangerous.

I was mindful of Evangeline's warning and didn't venture too close. I tossed a corn muffin toward the swans. They swam warily to where the soggy pieces floated, and nipped them up rapidly. I tiptoed over to the tree limb of the weeping willow and watched them.

Cobb was twice as big as his mate, the pen—I named her Penny Lane—like that Beatles song you always sang, Mama. Mr. Cobb had a thicker neck, the black knob above his orange beak bold and imperial. When the birds waddled out of the water, I noticed that his feet were black, while Penny Lane's appeared gray. Penny Lane followed Mr. Cobb everywhere he went, as did their little cygnets, who stayed close, often hopping onto Penny's back for a ride.

I wanted so badly to stay and watch them, but I figured

I'd best get back to the church before Aunt Bernie noticed my absence. She expected me to help clean up in the kitchen after social hour.

Moving closer to the edge, I held out another corn muffin for Mr. Cobb. Disturbed by my gesture, he swam closer, moving defensively, eyeing me with caution. I tossed muffin pieces to him, and he caught them neatly, crumbs falling into the water around him. Penny and the babies glided over and helped him devour them.

Mr. Cobb elongated his neck and bowed his delicate face my way, a thank-you of sorts. I left the rest of the muffins on the ground—an offer of friendship—and vowed to visit them again.

I hurried to the rear of the church building by the picnic tables, careful not to draw attention to myself. Loretta's voice reached my ears. I flattened myself against the back wall and listened.

"She not only tried to poison us with that pie, but she hawked an ice cube right at me, spit it directly into my face, right in our own house."

I crept around the corner and headed to the vestry door only feet away from where they were sitting. Matt Jensen noticed me. "Hey, dummy!" He lumbered toward me like a grizzly bear.

Lerman got up and followed him. "Well, if it isn't the ventriloquist's dummy."

They blocked my way, Lerman's face a wicked snarl. Matt and Jason loomed behind him. Loretta and Missy stayed at the tables, giggling like two nanny goats.

Lerman grabbed my arm. His fingers dug into my skin, his nails sharp as razors. "If I stick my hand up here"—his other hand threatened to go up the back of my dress—"can I make you talk?"

Jason said, "Lerman, that's enough."

Matt got his face right up to mine. "You need to apologize to Loretta."

Lerman pushed me toward Loretta, hand on my back, hard. As I stood my ground, he pushed harder, and I fell. I hit the gravel, tasting dirt, hard pebbles digging into my hands.

Suddenly Matt cried out, "Ow! What the . . ."

Faith's voice came from up above us. "Leave her alone."

I got to my knees and stood up.

Faith stood on the flat part of the roof, the cross behind her, her pitching arm back, a sizable piece of gravel in her hand. She aimed and hit Lerman right in the chest. He cried out in pain, too stunned to move.

Faith yelled, "Touch her again, and I'll take out your eye."

She dug into her dress pocket and threw a few more rocks, demonstrating the precision of her aim.

Missy and Loretta screamed and ran into the church, covering their heads.

Soon after, Reverend Love came busting out through the church doors. He was followed by a crowd of folks holding on to their Sunday Bibles and paper plates full of half-eaten food.

Faith continued to pelt the boys with insults and rocks. Some crouched under picnic tables or ran out of range. But Jason didn't move. He stood still, hands in his pockets, eyes down.

Reverend Love's face was red, his eyes wide.

He called, "Faith! Stop!"

He walked to the edge of the building, looking up at her, as mad as a badger. "Get down here. Now."

Faith shouted, "You tell those hick meatheads to back off and stop pestering Dulcie. Then I'll come down."

Reverend Love surveyed the faces of the remaining boys surrounding me. He picked up my Bible bag and handed it to me. "Are you all right?" he asked.

I indicated I was okay, but I glared at Lerman until he dropped his gaze.

Reverend Love spoke quietly through tight teeth.

"Matt, pew duty. Jason, you help. Lerman, clean the bathrooms. Now." He took a weary breath.

"Faith, come on down off there."

She stood still for a full minute, considering her options, then came down the way she'd gone up, by way of the rainspout, onto the metal trash container near the back entrance to the kitchen.

Reverend Love waved everyone inside.

"The show's over, y'all." He took Faith by the arm.

"What in the name of kingdom come were you thinking? Somebody could have been seriously hurt. The boys were wrong to be bothering Dulcie, but I can't have you being a vigilante around here."

Faith shook him off and walked into the church. She didn't look at me as she passed, ignoring me completely—as if she hadn't just saved my skin—as if she hadn't been magnificent, my very own avenging angel.

15

b-u-r-d-e-n

burden (n.)

anything that is carried; heavy load; the refrain or chorus of a song

When I arrived to sew choir robes with Evangeline the next day, Faith was already seated at one of the banquet tables. Evangeline leaned over her, head bent, gentle words floating, "That's right. Uh-huh. You don't have to hurry it. Take your time."

Faith unhooked scissors from her thumb and forefinger, and placed them down hard on the table. "I can't do it. I keep messing up."

Evangeline patted her hand, covering Faith's rough, nail-bitten fingers. "Child, we all mess up. We just got to keep trying."

Faith didn't look at me. In fact, she ignored me

completely. She picked up her scissors and scowled.

Evangeline threw out her arms and embraced me, like she hadn't seen me in a month. Maybe she'd had her fill of Faith's no-can-do attitude. "Dulcie, you are just in time. Faith and I cut out the rest of the robes this morning." She beamed, as bright as sunshine rays. "Faith was kind enough to come in extra early."

Faith gave me a miserable glance. "Preacher-man's idea. Crack-of-dawn punishment for making what he called an embarrassing display." Then she said, in a perfect Reverend Love imitation, "On a Sunday, no less. I appreciate what you were trying to do, but that wasn't the way to go about it."

She pointed at me, scissors in hand. "You owe me, big-time."

I dug into my Bible bag and took out my notebook. I pointed at the smiley face and showed it to Faith and smiled. I wanted to let her know I appreciated her taking on the Bible study bunch.

She shrugged. "They had it coming."

The bulletin from Sunday church service fell out of my notebook and floated to the floor. Evangeline picked it up and examined the cover carefully.

"A swan flying above Redeemer. Imagine that." She

gave me a sidelong look, saying under her breath, "You remember what I said. Those creatures are a thing of beauty, but dangerous, you hear." She handed the bulletin back to me, her face full of meaning.

Somehow she knew I'd been back down to the swan nest and was letting me know she knew. I tucked her warning, along with the bulletin, back into my bag.

Faith put down her scissors with a thump, finished with the robe she had been cutting. Her voice hopeful, she asked, "So, we done?"

Evangeline guffawed loudly. "No, child. Now we have to trace the patterns onto the cloth, and then we have to sew 'em."

Faith put her head down on the table and moaned. Evangeline's laugh, Mama, was warm and heavy, like syrup, and she poured it over you until you couldn't help but gobble it up.

Faith went back to work and shushed her complaining.

Evangeline showed us how to copy the dots and lines of the pattern onto the cut-out fabric shapes with blue tracing paper. We had to unpin the pattern from the fabric every few inches, and insert the tracing paper between the top and bottom cloth, and then run a little tracing wheel along the seam lines printed on the paper pattern.

When we took the tracing paper away, the markings were left behind on the fabric, so that we would know where to sew.

While we worked, Evangeline sang songs about freedom, going home, flying up to heaven, and one about somebody named John Brown.

> *The stars above in heaven now are looking*
> *kindly down,*
> *His soul's marching on!*

Faith recognized the tune and sang along.

> *Glory, Glory, Hallelujah!*

Her voice was high and sweet, a perfect accompaniment to Evangeline's low silky tones.

> *Glory, Glory, Hallelujah!*
> *His soul's marching on!*

Evangeline cast a glance at me. "Dulcie, you can sing along. Feel it in your body and let it free. Many ways to speak, sugar—not all of them with words. Some creatures don't need sound at all to communicate. There are ways under heaven to say what you got to say that are more natural than words can ever be."

I knew Evangeline was right, Mama. I thought about the swans—their secret language—how they spoke to me, and me to them—how we understood each other without words.

Faith and Evangeline continued singing. Using the tracing wheel to keep rhythm with their voices, notes sang out of my soul, and I made melody without a sound. I had only to imagine my voice rising out of me with ease, serenading right along with them.

Evangeline said, "That's it, girl. Don't let nobody tell you that you don't have a voice, when you can communicate just fine."

We worked until lunchtime. Evangeline brought out egg salad sandwiches and soda bottles from a metal cooler under the sink. We went outside to the farthest picnic tables by the playground, seeking shade.

Faith spread out on her back atop one of the tables. "Man, I am dog-tired." She ate her sandwich, looking up at the sky, her feet dangling over the edge.

Evangeline pried off the bottle tops with an opener, the kind Ray called a church key, and handed us each a soda. Evangeline laid out a cloth and some napkins, then sat, unwrapping her sandwich. I sat across from her.

Faith asked, "Miss Evangeline, you always been a choir director?"

She laughed. "Lord, no. Only since May. But it is my calling, I do believe." She took a swig of pop. "No, girl. I used to sew down in Atlanta, back in the day. I took in laundry, repair work, made dresses for people. Had me a husband back then too. We had a child. Things were hard for us, those days. Hard to get jobs. Hard to find a place in a world that didn't seem to want you, anyhow."

Faith sat up and crossed her legs. "You have a kid?"

Evangeline wiped some crumbs away with her napkin. With her voice low, and keeping her eyes down, she let the words rush out of her. "My baby's name was Jeremiah. When he was six years old, he opened up the screen door by himself. The puppy Jeremiah's daddy got him for his birthday ran out through it. Jeremiah followed that puppy right into the street, got hit by a car. He died in my arms, right in front of our house."

Evangeline laid her hands on the table, palms down, as if she were trying to keep her balance. She shook her head, as if by doing so she could keep something away from her that was threatening to overtake her.

Faith said what we were both thinking. "I am so

sorry, Miss Evangeline. I didn't mean to pry."

Evangeline looked out to the tree line and the field beyond. "I left Atlanta. I wandered here and there after that, settled in different towns, looking for a place to bury my hurt."

She took a stick of licorice root from her dress pocket and broke off a small piece of it. The smell was rich and crisp, lingering in the air around us. "I was so angry with God. I kept asking, 'Why did you take my baby from me?'" Evangeline popped the piece of licorice root into her mouth and chewed it as if it relieved her of calling forth her loss. "One day I found my way into a church."

She gathered up the wax-paper sandwich wrappers and folded them neatly.

"I started to sing. I went into that empty church every night, and I sang. I sang until I was hoarse. I sang even when I couldn't sing. One song at a time, I let go of the anger."

Faith's eyes were round black buttons. "This church?" she asked.

"Yes, this very church." Evangeline waved away a fly from the table. "But how I got here is another story for another time." Evangeline got up slowly. She patted Faith on the shoulder and went inside.

Faith and I lingered outside at the picnic table for a bit, soaking up the sun, letting the breeze tickle our bare feet. A ladybug landed on Faith's arm. She studied it for a while, then told it, "Fly away home. House is on fire. Your children are alone." She blew on it, and the insect took to the breeze.

Evangeline's story hung in the air between us, giving us pause, before we followed her inside. I understood then, the reason Evangeline knew the language of heartbreak so well, Mama. Though you would have never known it, she was near to drowning in it herself.

Back in the vestry, Evangeline said we were finished if we wanted to be. But Faith and I stayed.

We spent the afternoon singing, or as Evangeline said, letting go of our troubles. Faith's clear high notes, Evangeline's low smooth ones, and my silent ones—the rhythm of the sorrow inside us rising up in a chorus of glory hallelujahs.

16 〜

a-p-o-s-t-l-e

apostle (n.)

a person sent out on a special mission

Tuesday came—a whole week since I'd hit Loretta Swinson with my Bible. The day gave way to the glory of summer, the corn rising along with the heat. Evangeline had gone to town for sewing machine needles. Aunt Bernie was off to a Ladies' Auxiliary luncheon at Mrs. Butler's. Reverend Love had taken Faith to visit a county social worker to settle her paperwork.

I loaded up Maybelle with a couple of slices of Wonder Bread snitched from the bread box in the kitchen. Then I headed out for the pond and the swans. I pedaled down Victory Road, my heart lifted in anticipation, anxious to visit the birds and enjoy the quiet of their world.

When I arrived, the swans greeted me, swimming

close, observing me with care, protecting their babies from possible danger. After a bit, even the babies—the little pens and cobs—swam up, curious. I tore off little pieces of bread and tossed them into the water.

Penny Lane and Mr. Cobb held off from eating, letting the cygnets grab their fill. The parents were no doubt hungry too but remained watchful over the little ones as they enjoyed the feast I'd brought them. The cygnets stayed close to their parents and were often reminded to stay put with a tiny shove from Penny or Mr. Cobb. Some of the babies were bolder than the others, some greedier, some staying farther back. They seemed to have already grown a couple of inches since I'd first discovered them. Their bodies were rounder, their stubby pink legs sturdier.

When the bread crumbs were gobbled up, I climbed up onto the tree limb to watch them at their doings. The babies resembled ducklings, short-necked and stubby. Their wings resembled little appendages, without much worth. They didn't seem to mind that they weren't as beautiful as their mama and papa, though they imitated the way Mr. Cobb and Penny majestically preened their wings in the sunshine, flapping their downy baby winglets with pride.

Penny Lane waddled up to the shallows and paddled

her feet in a back and forth motion—loosening the plants and reeds from under the water. She nibbled here and there, waiting for the babies to do likewise, teaching them to gather the natural food within their reach.

After a bit, Penny and the cygnets toddled up to their nest, the large mound of sticks and leaves in the middle of the pond. Mr. Cobb swam nearby, guarding his brood—on watch—as the babies tucked their heads under Penny's wings.

Watching them made me ache, Mama.

Though I couldn't say it to anyone, missing you was like a fever that would come on all of a sudden, making me swoon with longing, my chest aching as if my heart had turned itself inside out. I had no control over it. I missed you so bad, Mama. I missed our life in Lilac Court. I even missed Ray.

Yearning crept up and lingered there with me. The trees sighed, holding me in their sway. The little splashes the swans made soothed me. I closed my eyes and imagined that I was curled up next to you—imagined that I had not left you that morning—imagined I had stayed with you—holding on for dear life.

Ray hadn't called or visited. He stayed away, as near as I could figure, because I was just a reminder of you and what had happened in the trailer that day. Sending me to Shepherdsville was the only way he could get on with living, I guess, not having to look at me and remember our life together.

When I lost you, Mama, I lost Ray, too. He was the only daddy I'd ever known. Now that you are gone, I'll never know who my real daddy is. You had promised that you would tell me one day, when I got old enough. Remember?

He could be somebody right there in Shepherdsville. Somebody I sat next to in church, or stood next to in line at Kessler's Drugstore. I couldn't help noticing every single man who might fit the bill—comparing him and me. Was his nose the same shape? Or his eyes the same color as mine?

I wondered if my daddy would know me on sight the same way I imagined Mr. Cobb would know his own swan babies, even when they were grown and had flown away.

I climbed down from the tree limb and wandered closer to the pond's edge. The water was murky, green with algae and little tadpoles. My hands were sticky with tree sap. I only meant to wash up. No sooner had I put my hands into the water than Mr. Cobb came at me like a bolt of white lightning.

He came right up out of the water at me—his wings spread full—hissing like a cat. He thought I meant his family harm, and he aimed to stop me. I took a couple of steps back, and he surged forward, flapping his wings.

I heard Evangeline's instructions in my head, how she told me to signal I meant no harm. "Now, if a swan were ever to get riled, you stand your ground. Hold perfectly still. You raise your arms out to your sides and hold them like Jesus on the cross. You act like a swan. Spread out your wings."

I lifted my arms out, stood still like a statue, and looked Mr. Cobb right in the eye. I tried with all my being to communicate with him. *I don't mean you any harm.* He remained in front of me, just a few feet away. He pulled his wings in, yet held his position. We stayed like that for a minute, until he got bored and went back into the water, ignoring me.

Shakily I walked to the edge of the clearing and looked back. Mr. Cobb paddled out to the nest, his long neck raised, as if to say, *This is my place. I make the rules.* He stuck his beak under the water and nibbled at the grasses as if he didn't care about me at all, but I knew he was still watching me closely.

I made my way to the parking lot and back to Maybelle,

breathless, legs quivering. If something had happened to me back there, no one would have known.

As I came around the corner of the church, I almost collided with the clothesline that Evangeline had set up from a hook on the church wall, by the vestry. The other end was fastened to a tree by the picnic tables. The last of the choir robe fabric was clothes-pinned to it—a rainbow flapping in the breeze. Evangeline sat in a webbed lawn chair, reading a *Life* magazine and sipping from a bottle of Coca-Cola.

"Well, Dulcie Dixon, where did you come from? Like to scare a person half to death."

I pointed at my bike. *Just out for a ride.* She wasn't convinced.

"What have you been up to?" She looked me up and down, taking in my mucky shoes and dirty hands. "You can wash up here."

She rose out of her chair and unpinned one of the long rectangles of fabric from the clothesline. "These are dry anyhow. You can help me fold, once you clean your hands. I'll press 'em and put 'em up in the vestry. You never know, our bitty choir might grow, then we'd have to sew us up some more robes." I knew Evangeline shouldn't count on that, Mama. The folks at Redeemer didn't strike me as a rainbow-wearing type of crowd.

I washed my hands in the vestry sink, then helped Evangeline take down the fabric. We folded it into a laundry basket and took it inside. Evangeline opened up the ironing board and plugged in the iron.

She bent over and got a Coke out of her old metal cooler and handed it to me. "You find something back there, you don't mention it to nobody, you hear? None of that wild pack down in the basement need to know anything about it. No need to mention it to your auntie, either."

I made the motion of locking up my mouth and throwing away the key. Evangeline looked sideways at me and guffawed. "Well, I guess we don't have to worry about that, do we?"

She touched the iron, making sure it was hot enough. "I reckon it's high time I tell you the story about the swan that brought me to Redeemer. Seems you've earned it. Being a swan-keeper yourself."

A *swan-keeper*. That sounded exactly right to me, Mama. I sat in the overstuffed chair in the corner, ready to listen.

She pressed the strips of bright cloth as she talked. "Years ago this would have been, before you were born. After I lost Jeremiah, I felt the need to move on. There wasn't much work to be had for a woman of color, and I didn't have much savings. I prayed and asked the Lord to send me a sign. I waited and I waited, but the Lord was silent. Nothing."

She glanced my way. "You listening?"

I nodded.

"So I took matters into my own hands. I went to the bus station and bought a ticket as far north as I could afford—to Chicago. But I only made it to Ohio, because the bus driver wouldn't let me use the bathroom on the bus. I had to wait until the scheduled stops. I put up a fuss, and he pulled into the station here in Shepherdsville and left me right in the parking lot. Tossed my suitcase out after me."

Evangeline sprinkled water from her ironing bottle, then smoothed the fabric, then sprinkled some more. After she ironed the cloth until it was smooth and shiny, she handed it to me to fold.

"I started walking from the bus station, flat broke, no idea where I was or where I was headed. My feet were plumb ready to give out. When I was sure I couldn't take another step, the Lord sent me that sign I'd asked for. A swan, wings spread wide, appeared in the sky above me, circling and swooping, guiding me straight to Redeemer Baptist."

Evangeline pressed and wiggled the tip of the iron down the length of the fabric, moving in long strokes, pressing it until she was satisfied.

"The pastor of the church at that time, Reverend Moore, was just locking up when I showed up. He saw me out by the parking lot and invited me in to rest my feet. After he gave me some tea, in this very room, he asked, 'You wouldn't know anything about looking after a church, would you?' and I said I thought I was up to that."

We folded the ironed cloth, each of us holding an end. "His housekeeper had passed just that month. She'd looked after the church for him too. I've been here at Redeemer ever since. When Reverend Moore died last year, he left me his house and put in his will that I was to always have a place here at the church."

Evangeline unplugged the iron. I moved to the floor and sat cross-legged, letting her have the armchair. She sat down and put her feet up on one of the metal chairs next to the table.

"When Reverend Love came to take over, he kept me on to look after the church. This spring he surprised me some and asked if I was interested in leading the choir."

Evangeline wrinkled her nose as if she could smell something not quite nice. "That's riled up a few folks, I gather, but for the first time in my life, I'm doing something I love doing. Music has lifted my pains and smoothed out the rough places, and if I can bring that to others, then it is my pleasure and my calling."

She patted the arms of the chair with both hands. "The good Lord meant for me to do it. That's why he sent me that swan. This old world is full of signs and wonder, if you pay attention."

The sun was starting to lean toward late afternoon, and Evangeline shooed me out, waving her hands. "You best get home before Bernice calls out the police. You come on and see me tomorrow morning. We'll get started attaching sleeves and sewing these up."

Back at the house, Aunt Bernie was making green bean casserole in her stocking feet. She would fry my butt like hamburger if she knew I'd spent the afternoon with a bunch of swans. Aunt Bernie was always after me about my *lollygagging* and would have pitched a fork into the hay if she'd known how close Mr. Cobb had come to pecking my eyes out.

Aunt Bernie put the casserole into the oven. She folded napkins on the table for supper, and then, as if she could read my mind like the Amazing Kreskin on television, she said as casual as you please, "Ray telephoned this afternoon. He's driving down to visit on Sunday."

Aunt Bernie and Reverend Love were always saying the Lord works in mysterious ways. I didn't know if it was true or not, but maybe Evangeline was right, Mama. The world *was* full of signs and wonders. I just had to pay attention.

17

c-o-n-c-a-t-e-n-a-t-e
concatenate (adj.)
linked together; connected

The heat wave in Shepherdsville continued with no letup. Aunt Bernie said it was drier than she could remember it ever being before—the earth parched, the cornfields browning. Everybody talked about the energy crisis nonstop—how we couldn't use electricity or turn on the fans because President Carter said not to. It was practically a sin to use an air conditioner.

Evangeline would have none of it. She had three fans going in the vestry, with two electric sewing machines set up on tables. "Lordy-be, it's hot." Sweat beaded on her forehead, shining like diamonds.

Over the next three days Faith and I settled into a routine.

We wrangled fabric into the clunky old sewing machines, doing our best to make neat rows of stitches, our feet pressed on the pedals. Evangeline showed us the trick of winding bobbins and how to keep the fabric flat as we worked. The air was thick as we poked multicolored threads through the eyes of needles and learned to run stitches up the clear tracks of the seam lines traced onto the cloth.

Evangeline taught us church hymns, folk music, and—best of all—Supremes songs. Diana Ross had nothing on Evangeline, Mama. Her voice poured into the vestry, as good as anybody on the radio. Faith sang along, rocking back and forth, playing a pretend piano—our own personal choir.

We sewed every day until lunchtime, then had sandwiches and Cokes at the picnic tables. Evangeline helped us pick dandelions and field violets and put them into tin cans for centerpieces, giving the rickety old outdoor furniture some beauty.

Every afternoon Evangeline called "quittin' time" when the heat became too much to bear. She would fold everything up, pack her cooler into the trunk of her beat-up VW bug, and putt-putt down the road, her rusty tailpipe talking back the whole way.

After Evangeline left each day, Faith headed upstairs to wait for Reverend Love, who worked in his office each afternoon, conquering his sermon for Sunday. I would wait fifteen minutes or so, hovering near Maybelle. When the coast was clear, I'd hide my bike in the bushes and head down the field and over the fence to Mr. Cobb, Penny Lane, and the babies.

I'd filched an old Tupperware container from Aunt Bernie's kitchen, and I would fill it with bread, cereal, or biscuits—anything I could stash away when Aunt Bernie wasn't looking. She made mention of my seemingly unending appetite. "Where do you put it all? My land."

The swans grew more comfortable with me, even seemed happy to see me when I arrived. Even though we were different species, I took this as a sign that we were becoming friends. They would greet me, pirouetting and dancing in the water like ballet dancers in unison, the little ones following, pattering in circles nearby.

Mr. Cobb became brave enough to eat out of my hand. I tossed the contents of the Tupperware to the rest of his swan family—who had become more courageous, more certain I meant them no harm.

Mr. Cobb patrolled his territory like a soldier when he wasn't feeding. Always distracted with mothering, Penny would let bread crumbs fall from her beak as she tended to her brood. Mr. Cobb and Penny remained on watch as the cygnets came closer to feed on the morsels I left them on the ground.

After a while I could tell the cygnets apart. I took out my notebook and drew pencil sketches of them, trying to capture their personalities.

There was a bold one with light feathers that I named Feisty. A smaller pink-footed finicky one, I called Trouble. The two who were always quarreling became Nip and Tuck, and my very favorite was little Lonely-Heart, the shyest of all.

They grew used to my presence, and we became accustomed to each other's ways. As the swans went about their business, sometimes I lay back, head on my Bible bag, with my eyes closed, listening to their tiny bustlings and occasional splashes. Once in a while I napped, dreaming of you, Mama—and Ray, or that I was at home at Lilac Court, or onstage at the spelling bee, words circling in my brain.

Sometimes my dreams got twisted up. Aunt Bernie would be in the trailer with us, or Ray would appear, preaching like Reverend Love at the pulpit at Redeemer. Evangeline appeared in the audience while I tried to spell out the word "cookies" and couldn't remember how to. Sometimes you sat with me on the porch of the farmhouse, not saying a word, pointing at your throat as if you couldn't speak either, and I would wake up in a sweat, my heart beating in my ears.

Friday afternoon, just as I situated myself into the tree limb with my notebook, Faith found me.

I sat up, startled by the sudden noise of the birds' rustling. The swans were out on the island nest when she appeared. Mr. Cobb's wings raised in alarm. He eyed her warily.

"Dulcie?" She didn't see me as she made her way into the clearing. I stiffened and froze, hoping she'd go away. Her voice grew louder. "Are you back there?"

I stood, angry to have been frightened—but most of all, disappointed to be discovered in the place I'd claimed for my very own. Faith spotted me and headed in my direction.

"What are you doing all the way in here?"

She blundered her way to me, the dry skunkweed scratching at her ankles.

"I thought I saw you go over the fence. What on earth . . ."

Mr. Cobb swam directly for the shoreline, his feet beating the water in a beeline toward her. He expanded his wings and approached Faith, meaning to throttle her good.

Faith's eyes grew wider as he got closer.

She squealed, "Eeeeeeeeeee!" like she was at a pig-calling contest, until I put my finger to my lips, signaling for her to pipe down.

I moved closer to her and motioned for her to stand as I was—still, arms extended wide. She did as I did, whispering, "Shoo. Go away. Go on. Please?"

Mr. Cobb lowered his wings and waddled over to me—protecting me, as if I were part of his territory.

Faith stood still, too afraid to move. Mr. Cobb flounced into the water, his job done. "Can I stop doing this now?" she whined.

I nodded, lowered my arms, and sat back down on the tree limb, waiting for my heart to return to its normal pace. She picked her way through the overgrowth and sat near the weeping willow. Faith assessed the place, taking in the light and the stirring of the leaves. Her voice was soft as her eyes swept over my secret place. "The swan nest. The one Evangeline talked about. This it?"

I nodded, but I sent her a message. *Secret, until now.* She held up her hand. "Don't worry. I won't tell anybody you were back here."

Faith rose and pulled long pieces of grass from the edge of the pond. When she had gathered a handful, she sat again and leaned against the base of the tree.

"Preacher-man told me to make myself useful. He's in there sweating over his typewriter. Wouldn't it be awful to have to come up with something to say to people every single week? Like that telephone game. Where you have to tell what the person next to you said. Except he's trying to tell everybody what God said, wondering if he got it right."

She wove the grass, overlapping the long strands into a green band. "I saw you taking off for the fence, and I followed you. I wondered where you were going. Thought maybe you were running away or something." She turned her head and looked up at me, teasing, "You're trespassing, you know."

I rolled my eyes. Faith spied my notebook. It had fallen to the ground when she'd startled me, my drawing of the swans smudged. "Can I see?"

She read the names of the babies out, sounding out the names slowly, squinting at the words with effort. I don't think Faith read much, Mama.

"Lonely-Heart." She pointed at tiny Lonely-Heart out on the nest. "The one that's at the tail end. All by herself?

Let's see. Nip and Tuck. Those two." They were easy to spot, pecking at each other in a constant battle.

"Trouble. That's the one who's plucking his feathers, and Feisty . . ." She pointed. "He's the one that's going back and forth." Her face softened. "You drew them real good."

Faith handed me back my notebook, the green woven band a bookmark in the pages.

We watched the swans for a while, the magic of the place releasing Faith's true nature—the sadness that floated around her like a rain cloud. I thought of her in the church basement and the night she had slept there alone. All of her toughness seemed to melt away here with the swans.

Penny circled up the cygnets and pushed them onto the nest. "That's the Mama, huh?"

I nodded, and wrote, *Penny Lane is her name*, in my notebook and showed it to her.

"Like the Beatles song?" She rocked back and leaned on her elbows.

After a bit she turned over onto her stomach and looked at me.

"Preach told me about your mama." She poked the earth with a stick. "About what happened."

Faith took a breath and revealed her own secret, saying it quick, like she had to get it over with. "I haven't seen my mom since I was, like, eight. She took off with some guy, and I haven't seen her since." She threw the stick into the tall grass. Hard.

"I don't forgive her. I hate her."

Her face darkened, splotchy places etched on her face. "I hate hating somebody I'm supposed to love."

Then, like an unexpected thunderclap, Faith broke into hard sobs. She rose to her knees and put her hands in front of her face, her shoulders hunched. I dropped down beside her and put my hand on her back. She shrugged me off and wiped her eyes, as tough as ever. "It's no big deal."

But I could tell it was, Mama. Her mother broke her heart and left her all alone in this world. Faith and me were more alike than I ever thought possible.

If the angels in heaven could have looked down, Mama, they would have seen us, kneeling by the water's edge, our sorrows sewing us together like Evangeline's glistening thread.

18

a-f-f-i-n-i-t-y
affinity (n.)
similarity of structure; family resemblance;
a natural liking or sympathy

On Saturday, Aunt Bernie planned a day of cobbler-making and Jell-O molding. The transistor radio in the kitchen, tuned to WGOD, played scratchy hymns. As I finished breakfast, Aunt Bernie pulled tins of flour and boxes of gelatin out of the cupboards, readying her weapons for an all-out assault on the taste buds of Shepherdsville.

A knock at the side door made us both jump, neither of us expecting company. Aunt Bernie dried her hands off on her apron. "Land sakes alive, who's come all the way out here?" She peeked through the window curtain. A sigh escaped as she opened the door.

Faith stood on the steps, in cutoffs and a T-shirt, a

man's handkerchief tied around her head. "Dulcie here?"

Aunt Bernie sputtered, "Well, she is . . . but . . ."

Faith whooshed past her, budging her way through the door. "Preacher-man drove me over."

Aunt Bernie eyed Faith as if she were a wasp that had gotten in. A wasp she meant to swat.

Faith winked at me. "We got big plans today."

Aunt Bernie surveyed my face.

I didn't know what Faith was talking about.

"Don't worry, Aunt Bernie. It's all on the up-and-up. We're going to the Bolt and Spool to get sewing needles. Evangeline needs 'em."

Faith scooted up onto the countertop and sat, grabbing a piece of bacon from the paper-towel-covered plate Aunt Bernie had left by the stove.

"Reverend Love took Mary to the doctor. She's been having pains."

A vein throbbed on Aunt Bernie's forehead. Faith knew just how to get into Aunt Bernie's good graces. A little gossip. She dangled information like a worm on a hook.

"Yep, she was feeling sick as a dog last night. Her ankles puffed up something awful."

Aunt Bernie took the bait, the worm wiggling all the

way down. "Poor thing. That baby is apt to come anytime now."

Faith jumped down and grabbed my hand. "Come on. Let's hit the road." She glanced at the Grateful Dead T-shirt hanging down below my knees. "Get dressed. Shepherdsville ain't ready for that git-up."

Aunt Bernie agreed with Faith. "Yes, please. Go on upstairs and change . . ."—she paused and let out a poof of air—"into something respectable."

Faith leaned against the counter. "So, she can come?" She arranged her face to pretend-seriousness. "I'll make sure she doesn't get into any trouble. I promise."

Aunt Bernie shook her head, aiming to say no. "Well . . ."

Faith made doe eyes.

Aunt Bernie bent and folded in the gale force of Faith. "Oh, all right, then. Get on with you."

Faith followed me to my room and flounced onto the bed. "I just made all that up. Last thing Evangeline needs is sewing stuff. I swiped five dollars off Preacher-man's dresser." She rolled onto her stomach, feet in the air. "Let's go spend it."

I tilted my head and bugged out my eyes, hoping she got my drift. *Juvie hall is your next stop, if you don't watch it.*

Faith pooh-poohed me. "Don't be such a worrywart. He won't even notice."

I opened the closet and pulled out one of Aunt Bernie's approved dresses.

Faith whispered, "Preach and Mary are a trip. Do you know they won't even kill flies loose in their house? They carry them out and let them go, saying they are God's creatures too." She poked a stick of gum into her mouth. "Asking all the time how I am, if I need anything, patting my head, making sure I brush my teeth, tucking me in at night, kissing my forehead like I was their real kid."

Then she muttered, "Thank God I'm not."

I don't think she was talking to me. It seemed to me she was trying hard to convince herself that even though she'd missed out on all those things in her own family, they were beneath her dignity. She pointed to the dress I'd pulled from the closet.

"God, Dulcie. You can't wear that dress. We're riding your bike. It's summer, for Christ's sake."

She slapped her hand over her mouth.

"Oops. Lord's name in vain."

I pulled the suitcase out from under the bed, Mama, and tucked your T-shirt inside. I found a pair of shorts and a tank top, and changed into them—then, for Aunt Bernie's sake, put the dress over them. I closed the suitcase and shoved it back under the bed. Faith toured the room, touching here and there, letting her fingers travel around my things—Aunt Bernie's Bible, my *Webster's*, finally landing on the spelling-bee cup full of words.

She squinted at the shiny plaque on the front of the cup: FIRST PLACE, ROSS COUNTY REGIONAL SPELLING BEE. She picked through all the words I'd written, and unfolded one or two of the tiny squares. "I don't even know what these words mean. You can really spell all these?"

I pulled my hair into a ponytail. *None of your beeswax.* I took the cup away from her and put it back. Those words were between you and me, Mama.

Your *National Geographic* collection and the map of the world on the wall caught her attention. Faith studied the map, letting her fingers trace the yarn you'd woven between the pushpins, creating patterns from here to there, places you hoped to travel to after you graduated high school and went to college. Places you never got to because I came along and ruined your dreams.

She peered at your name scrawled in pen on the desk blotter. "Emma Dixon?" I pointed to the picture of you and me, Mama, that I kept on the dresser. Her eyes widened. "This was your mom's room?"

She picked up the picture of us at Neon Beach in our bathing suits, our noses sunburned and freckled, your arm around me, our hair floating in the wind. She looked at me and put the picture down on the dresser. "You look like her."

Something unreadable played around the edges of her face. "Let's get out of here." She pulled the afghan off the foot of the bed and rolled it as neat as a jelly roll and tucked it under her arm. I grabbed my Bible bag and my notebook. We tromped down the stairs, our only obstacle Aunt Bernie.

When we reached the kitchen, she was stirring a bowl of green Jell-O in silence. She'd turned off the radio. "Just exactly how do you two expect to get to town? Do you want me to drive you?"

Faith waved her away. "Don't worry. We'll take Dulcie's bike. I can sit on the fender."

Aunt Bernie shook her spoon at us. "Don't go stirring up any trouble, now. Be back for supper, Dulcie."

She headed down the cellar steps to search her canned goods for the ancient fruit she stored in jars down there, most of it doomed to end up in her Jell-O molds.

Faith grabbed Aunt Bernie's transistor radio off the counter, fixing to take it with us. I gave her a don't-you-dare stare. Faith sure seemed to have sticky fingers, Mama. She rolled her eyes at me, then called down the cellar to Aunt Bernie.

"Hey, Miss Dixon, Dulcie wants to borrow your radio"—Faith paused, then smiled wickedly—"so we can listen to gospel music on our way to the Bolt and Spool. Okay?" Without listening for an answer, she burst out the door with it.

I hesitated, not wanting to rile Aunt Bernie. From the bottom of the cellar steps, I heard her reply, "My land, sakes alive. I suppose I can do without it for one afternoon. Best be careful now, you hear?"

I followed Faith out the door, before Aunt Bernie changed her mind.

We rolled Maybelle out onto the road, and after a few spills we managed a transportation method that worked. Faith sat backward on the rear fender, her feet dangling, while I wobbled and pedaled down the road. The tires squashed under our weight.

We made it up to the crest of the hill, near Old Tecumseh Road, and glided down the rise with hardly any effort. No cars passed us on the main drag into town.

After meandering our way through Shepherdsville, we arrived at the tiny filling station. Faith popped off the back. "Let's put air in the tires and get something to drink." I parked Maybelle by the side of the building, and we went inside seeking cooler air.

You must remember the old gas station, Mama? An old wooden building with a tin roof—two big windows in the front with a screen door in the middle. A saggy porch lurched underfoot, made out of planks and cement blocks. The man who ran the place, Bean, had filled up Aunt Bernie's car on occasion when we went to town, the empty sleeve of his shirt pinned up to the shoulder.

Aunt Bernie said he'd lost that arm in Vietnam. Though I tried not to stare, I was fascinated by how he managed to wipe our windshield and fill our tank using only one arm. Aunt Bernie would tip him a dollar, and he made a habit of saluting her with his good hand.

Bean didn't pay us any attention when we came in. He was deep in concentration, squinting at a Reds base-ball game on a small black-and-white television. Bean had dirty blond hair, floppy like a beach boy's, which made him seem younger than he was. His chin was scruffy with whiskers, his face handsome, despite his chipped front tooth.

Of all the men I'd seen in town so far, I had decided that Bean was my favorite choice for winner of my real-daddy contest. I had calculated it out. Our hair was the same color. He was skinny. I was skinny. His eyes were blue. So were mine. Plus, he was the right age.

Little prickles broke out down my arms. It could have been the window air conditioner blowing full tilt, or maybe it was like you always said, Mama. Those goose bumps were a sure sign that my guess was true-blue.

Bean continued to ignore us and grumbled at the screen, "Hell, that wasn't no foul."

Faith and I scouted out the gas station offerings: rows of candy, a few groceries scattered on the mostly empty shelves, dill pickles in plastic bags, beets and purpled eggs in jars, and a metal chest full of cold pop on ice. A tiny freezer held ice cream sandwiches and chocolate-covered bars on sticks.

Faith pulled out a couple of soda pops. I contemplated peanut-butter-and-jelly Goober. I grabbed a jar along with a loaf of Wonder Bread.

Bean yelled at the screen, shrieking, "He was SAFE! Moron. God. Dang. Moron."

Faith and I stood at the counter until we were noticed. Bean rose up to ring our sale, a solemn look on his face.

He regarded us with consternation. I wasn't sure if it was the ball game or if he didn't like customers in general. "If I had my arm, tell you what, I'd show those boys how to throw a ball."

He glanced over at me, inspecting me real good, sizing me up.

"You're Emma's girl, ain't ya, staying out with Bernie?"

I nodded. *Emma's girl.*

"Who's your friend?" Bean examined Faith. "Ain't seen you round here before."

Faith gave him the swiped five-dollar bill for the sandwich stuff and Cokes. "Just visiting," she said.

Bean deposited change into her hand, a couple of dollars and some coins. "Nice to meet ya, Just Visiting. "

He looked back at me. "Your aunt know you're running wild?"

I shrugged my shoulders, leaving him to guess the answer. He pointed a finger at me. "Don't do anything I wouldn't do." He smiled. "Or them good folks at Redeemer'll get you kicked out of heaven."

Bean closed the cash register and leaned forward on his elbow.

"You know that Russian guy that went up into space, first guy up there, you know what he said?"

I screwed up my face. *No, what?*

"Said he went all the way to heaven and he didn't see God up there." Bean laughed, enjoying himself. "No sign at all."

He pointed at his missing arm. "No God in 'Nam, that's for sure." He stopped himself, maybe realizing he was starting to sound touched in the head and we were getting spooked.

Faith gave me a nudge—a signal we'd better get out of there. "Let's go."

Bean smiled, his chipped tooth peeking through. "You take care, Emma's Girl."

As we gathered our stuff off the counter, the station bell dinged. Through the dusty window, we saw a red truck had barreled into the lot, going fast. It missed the pumps, then stopped, squealed, backed up, and swerved in next to the gas tanks, spewing gravel from the road.

Bean squinted, his eyes slanted against the light. "Aw, here's trouble." He picked up a baseball bat leaning against the wall behind him, keeping his gaze leveled at the gas pumps outside.

19

g-r-a-c-e

grace (n.)

a period of time granted beyond the date set for the performance of an act; mercy; clemency

Otis Burdine was at the wheel, harsh-faced, a John Deere hat pushed back off his creased forehead. His lip and jaw bulged with tobacco. He leaned out and spat a brown puddle onto the ground. Marlow wagged his tail in the back of the truck, tongue out, panting in the heat. Jason sat on the passenger side, his face a block of stone.

Otis shouted words, and Jason got out of the truck, his features contorted. He unhooked the gas nozzle and flipped open the little fuel door on the side of the truck. Otis slammed the driver's door shut and headed into the station. He swung open the screen door and brushed past us, the air suddenly thick with sweat and whiskey.

Bean's voice was even and steady. "You girls go on and take your Cokes outside." We headed for the door, staying as far away from Otis as space would allow.

Bean greeted him. "Otis."

Otis waved away the bat in Bean's hand. "No fussin' today, Bean. Just a pack of chew. Couple gallons of gas. The kid'll pump it."

Faith nudged me and whispered, "Let's go." We pushed out the door, antsy to be on the other side of it, away from whatever trouble Otis had in mind.

We headed for the air nozzle by the side of the building, where I'd left Maybelle. Jason filled the truck's gas tank at the pumps, oblivious as we walked past.

Faith arranged our Cokes and sandwich stuff with the afghan in the bike basket, then dug a couple of Snickers bars and five or six packs of gum from her back pockets. I pointed to the loot. I knew we hadn't paid for any candy and gum.

Faith said, "Well, he wasn't looking."

I gave her a hard look of disapproval. *I want no part of stealing stuff.*

Faith poked me in the ribs. "Don't be such a priss."

I let loose a puff of air from between my lips, the only way I had of expressing my exasperation with her endless pilfering. She was aiming for trouble, for sure, if she didn't stop pocketing what didn't belong to her. I knelt and unscrewed the cap from Maybelle's front tire. I took the air hose off the wall, and blew up the tire until it was good and firm. From the ground, I kept my eye on Jason, hoping he wouldn't notice us.

He'd left the pump unattended and had gone round to the back, to pet Marlow, who was whining for his attention. Jason leaned against Marlow, his head touching the dog's. He ran his hand gently down Marlow's scruffy ears and neck. Jason was so tender with that dog, I could hardly believe this was the same boy who'd been so cruel to me. By watching the two of them, I understood that Jason had little sweetness in his life, and what's more, I felt sorry for him because of it.

The pump clicked off. Jason pulled the nozzle out of the truck and went to replace it in the holster of the pump but missed, and it dropped onto the ground. When he picked it up, he accidentally squeezed the handle and gas spewed everywhere.

Otis staggered out of the building, clutching a pouch

of tobacco. When he noticed the gas that had leaked onto the ground, he sprang like a wild animal. He pounced onto Jason, jabbing him with his finger, over and over.

"Get in the truck. Can't you do a dag-gone thing anybody asks you without screwing it up?"

The screen door of the station opened with a bang, and Bean came out onto the porch, holding the bat. He called, "Move on out now, Otis."

Otis opened the driver's door, got in, and revved the engine. Jason walked around to his side of the truck, holding his arms at his sides like he was trying to keep all his parts intact. His gaze swept across the hood of the truck and found us.

Jason stared, appearing confused, maybe trying to calculate how long we'd been there—what we might have seen.

Faith shouted, "Take a picture, doofus! It'll last longer." I elbowed her hard. *Leave him alone.* Last thing we needed was more trouble with that crowd.

Jason slunk into the truck, and the Burdines pulled out, spitting dust. They rocketed down the road, old Marlow trying hard to keep his balance in the back.

Bean walked out to the pumps to check for damage, then turned and walked our way. He shook his head in disgust, then spat.

"Some people treat their kids worse than they treat their dogs."

The three of us watched the truck, weaving down the road, until it disappeared from view. Faith spoke, breaking the silence, "That's why they run away."

Bean looked at her sideways. "Just visiting, huh?"

"Yep," she said. Then she finished filling Maybelle's back tire and twisted the cap back onto the air valve.

Bean fumbled around in his shirt pocket, got out a crumbled cigarette, and lit it. His chipped front tooth made his smile appear sideways. He blew smoke rings neatly out of his mouth. They rose in perfect circles above my head. "It's Dulcie Louise, isn't it?"

Again I indicated that sure enough he had me pegged.

He leaned against the wall. "She was a good girl, your mama. Wasn't meant for this town, that's for sure. Folks talked quite a bit when she up and left."

He took a drag of his cigarette. "We were friends for a while, your mama and me. Heck—we were just kids." He let out smoke in a long stream that floated off in a wisp. "Yessir, I was sorry to hear how things turned out."

Bean looked off, not meeting my eye any longer. "Some things haunt you, ya know. Stick with you—crawl up inside and live with you. Sometimes you can't shake them, no matter what you do." He locked his jaw, far away in his thoughts somewhere.

My mind tumbled and turned, trying to unlock his meaning. I wasn't sure if he was talking about himself or you, Mama, but it hardly mattered. Bean knew who you were deep down, and more than anything else, I wanted to ask him a thousand questions. He spread the corners of his mouth into a toothy grin. "You come back and visit anytime, ya hear?"

Bean winked at Faith. "Candy bars on me." He went back inside, leaving Faith and me to our business.

Yep, Mama. Bean was definitely my number one pick for the could-be-my-real-daddy contest.

He didn't miss a trick. I liked that about him.

With Maybelle's tires sturdy with fresh air, we took off down the pike toward the church. We lit off through the field and made our lunch by the pond—Goober sandwiches from the gas station. The swans watched us eat, then nibbled our leftover crusts.

Faith spread out Aunt Bernie's afghan. We listened to Casey Kasem's top one hundred songs of the week on the transistor, while the swans circled in the pond.

Faith sang along with the radio, pretending she was singing into a microphone. I made drumsticks out of tree branches and hammered out rhythms. We ate the mushy Snickers bars and lay on our backs, studying the shifting leaves of the trees and the occasional drifting clouds. Faith took the wrappers off our gum sticks and folded the tiny papers into a colorful bracelet. She had a special knack for making something out of nothing.

She stopped her work suddenly and looked at me. "What Bean said, about some people treating their kids worse than dogs. If I tell you something, will you promise not to tell?"

I gave her a look of assurance. *Couldn't tell even if I wanted to.*

"I guess you can keep secrets better than anybody, huh?" She laughed.

She returned to work on her gum-wrapper bracelet. "He was talking about me, Bean was. What he said is true. That's why I ran away."

I listened to Faith, Mama, all that afternoon. She told me secrets about her life, and I can't tell you what they were, because I promised I wouldn't tell anyone. But I can tell you this—Faith's running away was the smartest thing she could have done.

While she talked, I drew pictures in my notebook—new pencil drawings of the cygnets, who kept growing more each day. After a while I started a portrait of Faith, while she wasn't looking. When I was almost done, she discovered what I was doing, grabbed my notebook from me, and scowled.

"You made me look . . . like somebody else."

I cocked my head. *What do you mean?*

"I don't know. You see me different. Not like most people see me."

Later that night I stared out at the moon, unable to sleep. Anxious for Ray's visit the next day, I'd managed nothing but an hour or two of twisting and twirling in the sheets. Finally I gave up and turned on the light. I opened my notebook and turned to the page of my unfinished picture of Faith. I took my pencil and filled in the missing parts, shading here and there, giving her dimension.

Then it hit me, Mama—why Faith looked different to me than she looked to other people—another secret

I'd known all that day but hadn't dared think out loud. There in Shepherdsville, I was the only person she had let see her. Really see her.

Without either of us looking, friendship had sneaked up behind Faith and me and tapped us on the shoulders, as unexpected as a perfect day.

20

v-i-s-i-t-a-t-i-o-n
visitation (n.)
the act or instance of visiting; migration of animals
or birds to a particular place at an unusual time or
in unusual numbers

Sunday morning I overslept, Mama. I dreamed that
you were waiting for me by the swan's nest behind the
church. You smiled like you had a big secret and couldn't
wait to share it. Your hair floated around your face, rising
in the wind, loose and carefree. I shouted—so happy to
see you that my voice came back, pure and strong. I called,
"Mama," and you lifted your arms out to me. When I
reached where you stood, you turned and flew away, giant
wings lifting you far above me. I wanted to go with you but
was bound to the earth and couldn't follow.

The sound of car wheels crunching gravel and doors

slamming outside my window woke me. Voices floated in on the morning breeze, dragging me awake, back to the farmhouse with the squeak of the screen door opening downstairs. Part of me lingered in the dream with you, craving to stay there. Aunt Bernie's voice crept in like fog.

"She'll be glad to see you."

Ray.

I sat up in bed, clutching the covers.

He had turned up after all.

I wasn't sure how I felt about seeing Ray, Mama—not certain if I wanted to bawl like a baby or kick him in the shins—repayment for leaving me there in Shepherdsville like he did. But then I thought about Faith and Evangeline and Aunt Bernie, and my thoughts got all twisted up like the sheets.

I hurried into the bathroom and ran water in the sink. When all the rust had run out of the spigot, I splashed my face. My reflection in the cracked old mirror stopped me. I'd never noticed your face in mine, Mama, until that very moment. Water dripped down my cheeks like I'd been crying. I wondered if I'd look this way when Reverend Love dunked me on Baptism Sunday—bleary and uncertain.

The sounds of scraping chairs in the kitchen and clinking plates made their way to me. Ray's voice vibrated in the walls, but I couldn't make out what he was saying.

Aunt Bernie came up and poked her head in. "Ray's here . . . and he has . . ." Her words dried up, her eyes darting away from mine. "Come on down. Your breakfast is getting cold."

I threw on a Sunday dress, one of Aunt Bernie's ladylike and appropriate-for-church numbers, clean white knee socks, and my shoes—still muddy around the edges from the pond.

As I started down, another voice halted me on the steps. "I can't wait to meet Dulcie."

A woman's voice. Ray hadn't come alone.

I grabbed the banister hard.

I didn't want to go down there, Mama.

Aunt Bernie fluttered at the bottom of the stairs like a loose bird in the house. She found me there, halfway up and partway down.

She trilled in her for-company-only voice, "Well, there you are. Come on down. Ray is here." Each step brought me closer to whatever it was I didn't want to know.

Ray leaned against the counter, sipping a cup of coffee. He looked at me, his gaze soft and steady. "Hey, Dulce." He had on a white shirt and some slacks, and his hair was combed. His shoes were even shiny.

He seemed crisp and solid. Real. I couldn't believe he

was standing in Aunt Bernie's kitchen. We didn't hug or anything. That hadn't changed about him, Mama.

A woman sat at the kitchen table. Her white-blond hair glowed—color from a bottle, and her eyelids were the shade of robin eggs. Everything about her seemed a little too bright, like staring into a light bulb. I almost had to squint to look at her. She wore an orange polyester dress that was shorter than Aunt Bernie would have said was decent.

Ray said, "Dulcie, this is Trixie."

Well, here it was, Mama.

Trixie. The thing I didn't want to know about had a name.

Suddenly I was transported to my bed in the trailer at Lilac Court, trying to sleep, unable to block out the sound of your voice shouting, "What's her name, Ray? I'm gonna call there right now!"

Trixie stood up and teetered over to me on long tan legs. Like a giraffe, she leaned down to me from what seemed an impossible height. She threw her arms around me and hugged me tight until I gasped for air like a drowning person.

She cooed in a baby voice, "Dul-cieeee, I am so happy to meet you."

She looked me up and down from under long eyelashes,

thick with mascara. "Aren't you the sweetest thing? Oh, Ray, you were right. She's just darling. Ray has told me so much about you."

I imagined myself saying, *"Well, he hasn't mentioned a thing about you, Trixie-bell. Not a word."*

Who has a name like "Trixie," Mama? Except maybe a horse.

I looked at Ray, and he glanced away, so I couldn't tell if my suspicions were correct—that this was what all your shouting had been about.

Trixie.

Aunt Bernie made a sound as if she might be choking on a chicken bone. "I'd best go on ahead to church to set things up. Miss Trixie, lovely to meet you. Ray, I'll go ahead in my car, and you all can bring Dulcie along with you."

I blinked hard, trying to imagine Trixie traipsing into Redeemer Baptist. There were likely to be heart attacks. Not many like her came down the pike around there.

Aunt Bernie picked up her pocketbook and was gone, leaving me with Ray—man of few words—and Trixie, who hadn't stopped talking.

"Well, you finish up your breakfast and we'll wait for you. We're looking forward to seeing the church where you've been spending so much of your time. Isn't that right, Ray?"

Ray winced like he had something to say but thought better of it. He picked up the Sunday paper, ignoring her altogether. He sat down and opened the pages, forming a curtain cutting himself off into his own Ray world, leaving Trixie and me to ourselves.

I sat, took a drink of juice, and fiddled with the eggs and sausage on my plate. Aunt Bernie had made a feast for forty.

Trixie picked up a sausage with her long pink nails. She bit into it and munched, smacking her lips. "Oh my goodness, that sure is good. We haven't had anything all morning." She poked Ray in the paper. "Come on out of there." She smiled like a beauty contestant. "He's checking gas prices."

Ray put the paper down. Trixie nodded at me. "Why don't you ask Dulcie how she's been doing, Ray?"

He took a gulp of coffee. "Christ, let it rest, will ya? She's doing fine."

Trixie put down the sausage and wiped her fingers on a paper napkin. "I'll bet it's a surprise—me being here with Ray. He offered to drive me down this way so I could visit my brother and his kids on the way back." She smiled with a sticky smile, smooth as maple syrup. "Isn't that right, Ray?"

I didn't feel like eating, Mama. I took my plate and milk glass to the sink. Ray looked at his watch and pushed back his chair.

"Better go see what the Holy Rollers have in store for us."

When we got to Shirleen's station wagon, Trixie and me silently tangled over who would sit where. She grinned and slid in next to Ray, forcing me to sit in the back. I slammed the door closed—as hard as I could. Neither of them said a word.

We cruised down Victory Road, looking like any other family in Shepherdsville on their way to church. Well, except for Trixie. Nobody would mistake her for a church-goer in that git-up.

I stared at the back of Ray's head, burning holes into his skull. The gall of him to show up after dumping me here, never coming to see me, and when he does, he's got a floozy in tow.

Ray picked up speed until the speedometer on Shirleen's old rattletrap read seventy miles an hour. I rolled my window down, hoping the wind would whip Trixie's hair into a whirl. She just laughed and rolled her window down too, holding her hair to one side to keep it from getting into her mouth. Trixie probably hadn't lived more than a minute of her life without making a sound. We hadn't gone far before she turned on the radio.

A song came on that was all deep tones and throbbing guitar—some guy singing about lighting his fire.

Trixie warbled along, her voice quavery and light. She was trying so hard to be likable, I almost felt sorry for her. I was trapped inside a cage with an exotic parrot who couldn't shut up.

Just as I was wishing to God she'd be struck mute too, Shirleen's old wagon sputtered, coughed, and died.

That's right, Mama.

We ran out of gas right next to a cornfield—too far to walk to church or back to Aunt Bernie's. Ray let out a flurry of swear words.

Trixie turned off the radio and gave him a mournful look, like she was as sorry as pie that he was going to get a piece of her feeble mind. She talked to him like a third-grade teacher. "Silly boy, I told you not to wait."

She looked over the seat at me. "He thought gas would be cheaper down here." She slapped him playfully on the leg. "Didn't have the patience to wait in line back in Columbus."

Ray sat, staring out at the road beyond.

"Well, what the heck are we supposed to do now?" Trixie stuck out her lips and pouted.

I knew one thing. We weren't going to make it to the church on time.

Hallelujah.

I was so happy at the thought of missing church, I spurted out a sound, air popping through my lips like bubbles. I clamped my hand over my mouth, I was so surprised to have made a noise. Trixie looked at me, alarmed, then snorted and laughed like a hyena when she realized I wasn't unhappy about missing church.

Ray looked at us like we were both crazy.

"Well, son of a gun." He got out of the car and stood in the middle of the road, hands on his hips, helpless. His shirt was wrinkled from the car seat. The junk he'd smeared in his hair gleamed in the sunshine. I suddenly realized he even had on a tie. That made me hate him a little less, that he'd dressed up for me, to come to church.

Trixie watched him through the windshield. "Ray don't laugh much."

We waited while he stood out on the road, kicking stones, his armpits getting stained from the heat.

Finally he relented and got back into the car. "Somebody will be along sooner or later, I guess."

We sat and watched the corn grow. Even Trixie was quiet.

After what seemed a month of Sundays, we heard a vehicle behind us.

It was the Burdines' truck barreling down the road, Otis at the wheel. Ray waved both his arms above his head, signaling them to stop. Otis slowed and pulled alongside Shirleen's station wagon. Jason and his mother were in the front, next to Otis, and old Marlow was in his usual spot in the back.

Ray got out and talked to them for a minute. Jason, who was on our side of the truck, fixed his gaze on Trixie. He'd probably never seen anything like her in his whole life. Jason stared and stared, glued to the sight of her.

Leaning in the driver's window of the station wagon, Ray gave us the news.

"This fella is going to take his family to church and then head on into Shepherdsville. He'll take me to the filling station there to get a gallon or two. Just sit tight. I'll be back in a few minutes."

Ray hoisted himself into the back of their truck, making room for himself next to Marlow. I wanted to yell out, *"Ray, don't you dare. Don't you dare leave me here alone in a cornfield with Trixie."*

But he did.

21

s-y-m-p-a-t-h-y
sympathy (n.)
sameness of feeling; affinity between persons

The sun beat down, turning the car into a hotbox. We baked, even with all the windows down, the cornfield buzzing in our ears. Trixie took off her high heels, peeled off her panty hose, and stuck them into an oversize plastic egg in her purse. She stretched out her legs and propped them up on the dashboard. What Ray saw in her, I couldn't tell you, Mama. She wasn't anything like you.

As if Trixie had read my thoughts, she shifted in her seat and looked at me, her big blue eyes like giant marbles.

"You must be wondering about Ray and me, huh? Maybe you've been thinking I'm trying to put my nose in where it don't belong?" She paused. "Well, I wouldn't blame you."

I turned away from her and concentrated on the telephone pole across the road.

"I mean, if it was me, I'd be worried about somebody coming in to take my mother's place."

"*Trixie,*" I wanted to scream, "*just cram it into your piehole.*" I continued to stare hard at the telephone pole, hoping it would fall over on her.

"Well, I don't want you to worry about that. We're just friends, is all. He comes into where I work sometimes— the Crystal Pistol on Highway 70? He's going through a rough patch, just like you. He comes in a lot, sits at the bar, and I listen."

I'll just bet.

Trixie dug around in her purse and brought out some lipstick and a compact. She reapplied the tangerine color to her lips, then patted herself on the nose and around her face with powder.

"Oh, God, it's sizzling. I'm practically melted." She stowed all her paraphernalia away, and without warning, crawled right over the front seat into the back with me.

Trixie stretched out her long legs again and propped her feet up, wiggling her toes in the air. "He talks about your mother all the time, you know, and about you, too. That man loves you to pieces, like you were his very own."

She patted my knee. "I know he has a hard time showing it, but he's afraid of losing you, too. If he shows how much he cares, he'll bust into tiny little pieces. Just give him time." She ran her hand alongside my head, gently. I jerked away.

She took a brush out of her purse. "Here, let me brush through those snarls." She turned me around and tried to comb through the mess the wind had made of my hair. It was no use fighting her. She was determined.

"I'm real sorry about what happened to your mama. Sorry for you, and for Ray, too."

She continued to brush, and I relaxed against her. "I didn't know your mama, but I talked to her a few times. She would call up to the Crystal Pistol looking for Ray. We'd get to talking late at night, about this and that while she waited for Ray to show up. She was funny as all get-out, your mama. She made me just pee my pants sometimes. And she always said the same thing when we got off the phone. 'Gotta go check on my kid. I like to watch her sleep, always have, ever since she was a baby.'"

Right then, it was as if Trixie had the key to a locked door that needed to open, and when it was unlocked, everything trapped inside me came rushing out.

Then I let Trixie, of all people, hold me while I let go

of what I'd been holding on to all those weeks—what you used to call an Ugly Party, streamers of snot and cups of tears.

When I was done, she gave me a lace hanky from her purse. I blew my nose, sat up, and smoothed my skirt.

"Here, let's fix you up a bit," Trixie said.

She finished brushing my hair, then got out her compact and patted my nose and cheeks with pale powder.

"Better?" she asked. I gave her a signal that I was closer to fine. I wasn't even embarrassed.

I don't know how Trixie did it, but all of a sudden she was the kind of person I imagined I could talk to. I could even see why Ray might seek her company, or how you would've confided in her, Mama. She had that effect on people; it was her special talent, instead of, say, pie baking or piano playing.

Right then I wished the words would come back so that I could really talk to Trixie about you, Mama. But the lump in my throat wouldn't have let me, even if I could tell her all of it—how I wished I hadn't gone off to win a stupid spelling bee, how it was my fault you turned on that oven.

Before long the Burdines' truck rumbled down the road and pulled up next to us.

195

"Well, hallelujah!" Trixie shouted out the window. She got out and repositioned herself in the passenger seat in front. "The Lord *is* with us."

She turned around and winked at me.

Ray hopped out of the truck. On the way back to the car, he patted Marlow on the head. Then he tipped gas into the tank from a beat-up gallon can, popped into the driver's seat, started the car, and waved Otis Burdine on.

We drove to church. Trixie turned the radio back on and sang along. This time I didn't mind as much.

Ray pulled into the parking lot. Otis Burdine finished tying Marlow up to his truck, then proceeded with his usual routine of sitting in the truck, sipping something out of a brown bottle, before he joined his family for the Sunday service.

Through the open church windows I could hear voices rising—*praise God from whom all blessings flow*—rising from the rafters.

Ray decided he and Trixie should go back to Shepherdsville—return the fuel can to Bean at the filling station and then gas up the station wagon. They promised to meet me after services at the social hour downstairs.

Ray opened my door. "Your aunt Bernie is having a conniption right about now, so you best get in there."

I crept into the back of the church. I'd missed Reverend Love's sermon, which was fine with me, as he was apt to be long-winded. Mrs. Wheeler, the organist, played a hymn as the collection plate was being passed. Evangeline and the choir members who had decided to show up sat in their places up front.

Jason Burdine and his mother were settled midway up the church aisle at the end of a pew. I spied Faith sitting kitty-corner in the opposite row. I tried to make my way over to her without drawing attention to myself, but that was impossible. Disgruntled folks stared with disapproval at my late arrival.

I scooched in at the far end of the same row as Faith, her on one end, me on the other. The Swinsons were across the aisle in front of the Burdines. I watched Mr. Swinson make a big deal of taking out his money clip. With a flourish he dropped a twenty-dollar bill into the collection plate, and passed it on.

That was when I wished I'd never made it to Sunday service at all.

I'd gotten to church just in time to see Faith holding the collection plate after she'd received it. She let it sit in her lap before it got picked up by the collection takers. She didn't notice anybody watching her.

But at least two people were watching.

Jason. And me.

Faith didn't see our eyes meet.

We both had seen the same thing.

Faith had stolen Mr. Swinson's twenty right out of the collection plate.

22

b-e-n-e-d-i-c-t-i-o-n
benediction (n.)
an invocation of divine blessing

The service ended, and I bolted out the back, avoid-ing any contact with Faith. My heart was beating the same thing over and over. *Why did she do such a stupid thing?* What would Reverend Love do if he found out she was stealing from the church?

The day was hot and breezy, like devil's breath. People clustered outside to speak to Reverend Love, wiping hair out of their eyes or holding on to their hats. Some headed to cars for home, hurrying off to hunker down in front of an air conditioner—no matter what President Carter said. Some braved the heat and descended into the basement for refreshments and a sure case of food poisoning, with all those salads left out.

I sidled away from the line of well-wishers and headed for the tree line past the cemetery. Evangeline was at the far end of the graveyard with a basket, standing among the gravestones. She waved me over.

"Sugar, your aunt Bernice was worried as a toad under a harrow about you."

I had no idea what a harrow was, Mama, but it didn't sound good.

She patted my arm and gave it a squeeze. "You best let her know you're here. Ready to call the sheriff, I reckon. Thought you'd run off with that Ray fella without telling her."

Evangeline squinted at me. "You look plumb frazzled, child. Let's get you a cool drink." She guided me alongside her as we walked back toward the church.

"I come out here sometimes and pull the wildflowers and weeds away from the stones—clear off the names, so people can see 'em."

Evangeline stooped and brushed off the top of a tottering old gravestone, her fingers brushing it lightly as if it were a precious thing. "Somebody loved each and every one of these souls. Seems a shame for them to not have visitors, so I come and let them know they aren't forgotten." She handed me the basket of wildflowers—little blossoms of yellow and purple. "You carry these for me. We'll put them in water." She pulled one last bunch of wild stalks away from a grave marker.

"I don't know where my Jeremiah is buried. They put him in a county grave somewhere."

Evangeline stopped in front of a stone that had one word on it:

WILLIE

She waved her hand over the grave. "Everybody needs a place where they can visit those who have passed on, so I imagine Jeremiah is right here."

I thought about the Littleton Funeral Home box still on the mantel at the farm, Mama. It didn't seem like the right place for it, but both Aunt Bernie and I avoided the task of finding a better spot.

I carried the basket of wildflowers and held on to Evangeline's elbow. She greeted people as we walked, saying, "Glory be to you," and "Have a glorious day."

Most people were polite and greeted her back, while some veered off if they saw her coming—as if a divide as big as the Grand Canyon ran right up the cracked sidewalk.

At the side of the building, I spied Jason talking with Reverend Love. Jason's face was red and animated like a cartoon bull's. I couldn't hear him, but no doubt he was squealing on Faith—about her stealing the Swinsons' money from the collection plate.

I followed Evangeline into the vestry. She turned on the sink and let it run so it would be real cold, and poured me a cup straight from the spigot. I gulped it down, something earthy and rich rendering the water delicious. I filled up another and drank it, too.

Evangeline got out a mason jar, filled it with water, and arranged the flowers under the Every Good and Perfect Thing sign. Without any prompting from me, she pointed at the small handmade plaque. "My boy made that for me. Only thing I have of him." She put the basket under the sink and said nothing more about it.

The new rainbow choir robes were hanging on the rack waiting to be hemmed. Evangeline reached up and pulled out a white cotton robe on a hanger. "This is your robe for Baptism Sunday."

It seemed like a million years ago that I'd agreed to such a thing—dressing up in a white gown, only to be dunked into a tub. Now it didn't seem there was any way out of it.

I reached out and touched the fabric. It felt soft and billowy under my fingers.

"We'll hem it up for you this week." Evangeline smiled. "You go on and let your aunt know you're here."

I headed down to the basement. People stood around with paper cups of coffee, napkins filled with lemon bars, plates of ham and potato salad. Aunt Bernie was helping Mary Love in the kitchen and didn't notice me as I walked by the pass-through. I headed in her direction to let her know I'd arrived, no worse for the wear.

Hands clasped over my eyes.

"Guess who?"

I whirled around to face Faith, and glared. *I am so mad at you.*

"What?"

Reverend Love appeared beside us. "We missed you this morning, Dulcie. I understand you folks had some car trouble on your way to church." He laughed. "Well, I'm glad you made it for the important part." He winked at me. "The Jell-O and pie."

He turned to Faith, his expression unreadable. "Faith, could I have a word with you?"

"Sure, Preach."

She followed after him, calling out over her shoulder, "Wait for me, okay?"

I had no way of warning her that she'd been caught,

that Jason had spilled his guts. Maybe she deserved what she had coming, but I hated that Jason had put her in hot water.

I could only hope that Reverend Love would understand the mixed-up thinking behind her stealing money from the collection plate, but I doubted it. He'd given her a chance, and she had blown it for herself.

As the last few people were heading out to their cars away from the basement and the heat, Ray and Trixie wandered in. They made their way over to me. Trixie stuck out like a full circus had come to town. Ray pulled at his collar, uncomfortable to be in the midst of the church crowd.

He whispered as if God himself could overhear, "Trixie and me need to head out. We've got a long drive ahead and some visiting with Trixie's people, so we best get on the road." Clearly, Ray had had too much of Shepherdsville, Mama, and was cutting out before we had time to figure out we missed each other.

Trixie gave me a little pat, her voice sincere. "Dulcie, I am *so* happy we got to know each other." She dug into her bag and handed me her pink plastic compact. "You know, just in case."

She nudged Ray. "I'll wait for you outside. My dress is already pit-stained enough as it is."

Ray cleared his throat. "I'll be back down soon. I don't know when." He sputtered a string of things, trying to put them together. "I got . . . stuff to do . . . take care of . . . and you seem settled in here all right. Everything is okay, isn't it?" He swallowed. "I mean, you understand, I can't . . ." He stopped, his words drying up.

I put my arms around his waist and held on to him, tight. It was the only thing I could do for him, Mama. It took him a long time, but Ray put his arms around me too. We stood like that until I could feel his chest starting to buck like a wild thing.

He turned and left me there in the stairway—with Aunt Bernie and a basement full of discarded napkins and dirty dishes waiting.

When she found me, Aunt Bernie lighted on me like a pesky fly. "Heaven's sake," is all she said. She handed me a dish towel and apron, and I went to help her clean up.

23

t-e-s-t-i-m-o-n-y
testimony (n.)
public avowal, as of faith

I was elbow-deep in dishwater when Reverend Love sent for me, Mama. Aunt Bernie took the dish towel from my shoulder. "You run along. I'll finish up."

Plodding slowly up the stairs, I could feel my heart drumming a funeral march. My hands oozed, hot and sweaty, as if I had a coal furnace in my chest. I could barely breathe. The wood floors creaked under my feet as I walked softly down the hall to Reverend Love's office. I knocked on the glass part of the door—a rattled chord under my knuckles.

Reverend Love opened the door, his face grim. "Come on in, Dulcie."

Hurt feelings and uncomfortable words hung in the

air. Jason and Faith sat on opposite ends of a ratty sofa inside Reverend Love's office. Faith's arms were crossed in front of her chest, her face dirty with a scowl. Jason leaned forward, lips pursed, elbows on his knees, staring at the floor.

Reverend Love took a seat behind his desk and indicated I should sit. The only place available was between Jason and Faith. I sat and tried to catch my breath. All the oxygen in the room seemed to have been sucked away.

"Dulcie, I need to ask you something, and I'd like you to tell the truth. Then Faith and Jason can come to an agreement as to what might have gone on today in services."

Reverend Love leaned on his desk, one hand cradling his cheek, holding his head up, as if it were too heavy to stay upright by itself. I got the impression that what had been said in that office was a disappointment to him.

"Now listen, Jason and Faith, you both know that stealing is against the law. If you break the law, you end up a criminal. I know this to be true. I can't let either of you go down that path."

He softened. "Faith, tell me again what happened today."

She glanced at me, then back to Reverend Love.

"Jason Burdine hates me, and he told a big fat lie. He's the one who stole the money."

Jason yelled out, "I did not. I watched you take it out of the collection plate and put it in your pocket. Don't try to pin this on me."

He swiveled toward me, his voice rising. "You saw her. We both did."

Faith pleaded, "You didn't see me take any money, did you, Dulcie? You saw Jason do it. You were sitting right there. You must have seen him."

Reverend Love rubbed his forehead. He scanned my face, searching deep down to my very soul. "Dulcie, did you see Faith steal money at services? Did you see Jason take something from the collection plate?"

Mama, you raised me right. I know the Ten Commandments. *Thou shalt not steal. Thou shalt not lie. Thou shalt not . . .* Well, I don't know all of them, but those two stuck in my head.

I didn't want Faith to get in trouble. Jason, on the other hand, had made my life miserable since I'd arrived in Shepherdsville.

Reverend Love waited for an answer.

Before I had time to consider what I was doing, Mama, I sinned right there in Redeemer Baptist Church—probably a double sin, because I lied to a minister of the Lord.

I looked Reverend Love right in the eye and pointed at Jason.

Reverend Love winced. "Jason stole the money from the collection plate?"

I nodded. Jason's jaw dropped. "I did NOT."

Faith shouted back, "You did too."

Jason lowered his voice to practically a whisper. "She's lying."

Reverend Love returned his gaze to me, looking at me hard for a long minute, while I squirmed, sweat popping like blisters on my skin. I dropped my eyes, not sure I could go through with being a snitch. A lying snitch, at that.

"Are you sure, Dulcie? God is listening right now. He would not want you to lie to protect a friend. Are you sure?"

I nodded, a hard lump, a rock of regret lodged in my throat. Faith had stood up for me, and now I was standing up for her. It felt wrong, but I had to do it, Mama.

Reverend Love stood up. My queasiness rose along with him. "All right, then. Dulcie, you can go. Faith, wait outside for me."

Faith followed me out into the hallway. She grabbed my hand and whispered, "Thanks. It'll teach that yokel to not mess with us." I shook her off, hopping mad at myself for lying and as frustrated as a bug under a jar at her for putting me in the situation at all.

Otis Burdine and his wife waited by the front door. Reverend Love called them into his office. "Jason's got something to tell y'all. Come on in."

Passing them, my cheeks on fire, I rushed out of the church to the porch. Almost everybody was gone by then, the parking lot empty of cars, save for a few: Aunt Bernie's Olds, Reverend Love's wagon, the Spanglers' rusted-out Dodge, and the Burdines' truck. Marlow was sprawled out beside the truck, his eyes looking mournful, miserable in the heat.

Gray haze moved in—even the sky seemed to have caught on to my mood. I should have gone back up there and told Reverend Love the truth—that Faith and me were both sinners. She was a thief, and I was a liar.

Faith trailed me to the porch and stood behind me. "Thanks for saving my butt," she said. "I'll have to clean the place from top to bottom this week and dust all the pews, but I'm not going to be nailed to a cross or anything."

She bounced down the steps to the lot, gathered gravel from the ground, and tossed stones from one hand to the other, shifting them back and forth, like a juggler.

"Look, Jason is a punk. He deserved it."

I refused to look at her.

"Dulcie, come on. It's no big deal." She sidled up in front of me. "I'd have done the same for you. You know I would have."

I turned and stomped back to the church doors. She followed, intent on changing my mind.

"Dulcie, wait."

Exasperated, I whirled and shot her all of my ill temper. I conjured lightning bolts flying out of my eyes and venom shooting out from my gritted teeth. At least, that was what I hoped I looked like—the devil on a bad day.

"Dulcie!" She grabbed my arm, desperation in her voice. "Come on. Don't be mad."

I closed the sanctuary doors right in her face.

The quiet of the church echoed my footsteps as I passed the pews on my way to the vestry door. Evangeline was gone. The cemetery flowers she'd picked for her son sat, bright and hopeful, in the silent room. The white baptism robe hung on its hanger, waiting for me.

The heavy pinch of what I'd done to Jason throbbed in my chest. I hadn't wanted to let Faith down, but I shouldn't have lied to protect her. I'd let Reverend Love down too. He had put his trust in me and I'd pointed at the wrong person. Aunt Bernie would want to strangle me if she found out I was nothing but a liar.

Poor Jason. Sure, he had been mean to me, but he didn't deserve punishment for something he didn't do.

The sign Evangeline's son had painted, the scripture carefully written in black paint, rested in its place on the shelf above me: "Every good and perfect thing is from above."

One day, when we'd been sewing together, Faith had asked Evangeline what the scripture meant. Evangeline was piecing together fabric, pins in her mouth. She took her time answering, but when she did, she leaned forward, placed her hand under Faith's chin, cupping it, and looked deep into her eyes.

"What it means, sugar, is that when we fall—and, oh, honey, how we are going to in this life—we have to fall looking up. That's all you gotta do. Look up. Find a way to rise up, even when you are flat on your back. That's what it means." She turned away and busied herself with stitching, needle going in and out of the fabric like a silver dart.

Faith shrugged. "What if you can't get up, no matter how hard you try?"

Evangeline said, "You ask for a hand up, and go on the best that you can."

As I sat there, alone in the vestry, after I had lied to Reverend Love, Evangeline's words, like her neat stitches, one after the other, in perfect order, led me to the answer. It was right in front of me, Mama. I knew what I had to do.

Your suitcase waited under the bed. Everything I owned would fit into it. I had Maybelle—she could get me out of town. Faith had told me how she'd managed to get from place to place, tricks she'd used to travel on her own—what to tell bus drivers so that they'd let you on the bus without paying. The best places to catch rides—churches and schools. How to wash dishes for a meal.

It was clear to me, Mama.

Me leaving Shepherdsville was the best thing for everybody. Maybe Ray didn't want me, but I could take care of myself back at the trailer.

My Bible bag was right where I'd left it, on the over-stuffed chair by the wardrobe. I reached inside it and pulled out the crumpled Sunday bulletin from the service the week before, the swan that I had drawn on the cover flying over Redeemer Baptist. I thought maybe Evangeline would like it. So I placed it next to Jeremiah's sign on the shelf there in the vestry. I dug out my smiley-face notebook from the doctor and opened it. My drawing pencil was tucked inside, ready for the words I needed to say.

Lilac Court waited for me. It was where I belonged.

But first I had to do something.

24

c-o-n-f-e-s-s-i-o-n
confession (n.)
an admission of guilt, especially formally in writing

Dear Reverend Love,

By the time you get this, I'll be gone from Shepherdsville for good. I know you and Aunt Bernie both tried to help me, but it's no use trying any longer.

I did the wrong things for what I thought were the right reasons, but the reasons I did what I did don't matter now. There are some things you should know.

First off, I lied about Jason. He didn't steal the money from the collection plate. Please don't be hard on Faith. She has a hard time asking for a hand up.

And I sort of lied about something else, too. Remember the night I hit Loretta with my Bible? How you told me about the swans?

Well, I did see one, that very night, flying over Redeemer. I don't know why I didn't let you in on the truth. When you told Evangeline we'd been swan-watching and that we hadn't been lucky enough to see one, I went along with it. I guess I wanted to keep the swans to myself. But keeping things to myself lost me my mama.

Not saying anything, sometimes, is worse than telling a lie.

Sincerely,
Dulcie Louise

P.S. Tell Evangeline I'm sorry about not being here to help finish the robes.

My pencil lead broke, I was pressing so hard on the paper.

But it was done.

I tucked the note into the pocket of Reverend Love's preaching robe that was hanging on the vestry door. He wouldn't find it until the next Sunday, and by then I'd be long gone.

I planned to pack up when I got back to the farm and leave after Aunt Bernie went off to do bookkeeping at the radio station the next day. I aimed to leave her a note too. I would tell her not to worry, that I was going someplace safe.

Ray would be out on the road where nobody could reach him. He wouldn't know I'd left Shepherdsville until he got it into his head to call or visit me at Aunt Bernie's. Maybe months. Maybe never.

I figured that no one would bother to look for me at Lilac Court. Your tip jar was still hidden behind the water heater, Mama, and I could use it to get along by myself for a while. If Faith could manage on her own, so could I.

The quiet was broken by a sudden ruckus going on. Old Marlow was yowling up a storm outside. From the vestry it sounded like he was trying to call the dogs in the next county. He barked angry yaps, followed by long wailing howls.

I opened the vestry door to the outside and followed the noise around to the front of the building. Shouting joined the dog's voice. When I got to the parking lot, I stopped, the scene in front of me so brutal that I wanted to look away, but couldn't.

Otis Burdine had Jason up against the truck, smacking him around the top of his head, punching him in the arms, slamming his body against the truck door like he was a rag doll. Jason crossed his arms over his head, covering his face, but could do little about the rest of his body. He drew himself up into a ball, protecting himself the best he could from the blows.

Otis threw Jason to the ground, hollering and railing, "I've had enough of you. You're nothing but trouble, you hear me. I will teach you a lesson if it's the last thing I do." Foam flew from Otis's mouth. "You steal from a church, you no good, worthless . . ."

Mrs. Burdine stood, frozen, clutching her purse and her Bible, eyes wide, huddled on the other side of the truck, weakly calling, "Stop it, Otis," over and over, afraid to come nearer, else she get hit as well.

Marlow jumped and pulled at his lead, trying to reach Jason, who had sunk to the ground, his back against the truck, a small ball of misery.

Otis kicked him. "Get up, you baby."

My nails dug into my palms. I leaned against the side of the building, my legs shaky and quivering. Dots of light floated in front of my eyes.

I had caused this. It was my fault, Mama.

A sound shook the porch as if a bolt of lightning had cracked the sky. The sanctuary door opened with such force, the bell next to it rang out a clear tone. Reverend Love's long legs carried him down the porch steps, two at a time, and out to the Burdines' truck in one swift motion.

Reverend Love grabbed Otis by the collar hard and pulled him away from Jason, his voice tight. "Leave. Him. Alone."

Reverend Love stood, nose to nose with Otis, his breath coming out in windy gasps. "Don't touch him again."

For a mostly mild-mannered preacher who talked about love and peace on earth, Reverend Love sure looked like he could whup butt, if need be. His whole demeanor changed right before my eyes—into somebody who knew how to fight and use his fists, somebody who'd had his share of scrapes and brawls.

"Get into your truck and leave, or I will the call the police, do you hear?"

Otis backed up, unsteady on his feet, shamed like a dog with his tail between his legs.

Keeping his eye on Otis, Reverend Love extended his hand to Jason. "Jason, go on inside." Reverend Love pulled him to his feet and whispered something into his ear. Jason nodded, his eyes on the ground.

Otis untied Marlow and pushed him into the truck cab. He backed up, slammed on his brakes, and lurched out onto the road, tires squealing.

Missy Spangler's mother, Carol, was on the porch, holding a platter, having happened upon the whole thing, her mouth a round O. Reverend Love guided Jason to his mother.

"Jolene, take him inside. Get him cleaned up. Have Carol take you over to your mother's place. Let Otis sleep it off. I'll stop by tomorrow, see if we can't get him sorted out, get him over to the county tank to dry out."

Mrs. Spangler and Mrs. Burdine helped Jason inside. A small trickle of blood ran down his face from a split eyebrow.

I leaned against the church, hidden in the shadows, my knees weak, frozen in place.

After the others had gone inside, Reverend Love sat down on the front steps, jacket ripped, hair falling over his eyes. He leaned his head on his knees, motionless. I couldn't move. I watched him, afraid to leave for fear I'd make a sound and draw attention to myself.

He sat, his head in his hands. He stood up after a bit and kicked the edge of the porch hard with his shoe. His voice reached me, a hoarse whisper. "Hell's bells."

I wanted to go over to him, tell him it was all my fault—all of it. He didn't need to worry. He was doing his job just fine. If the big man upstairs was mad at anybody, it was me, not him. I was the one who hadn't told the truth.

Just like I was the one who hadn't told Ray about you, Mama. And how I was the one who told Mrs. Whitehouse, the morning we left for the spelling bee, that nothing was wrong when she asked, "Honey, is your mama okay? She didn't look well."

I lied, Mama, and said, "Oh no, she's fine. She worked late last night. She'll be okay as long as she rests."

Not telling had caused nothing but trouble.

Maybe I could have changed things if I'd told Ray how scared I was, or if I hadn't pretended to Mrs. Whitehouse that you were fine. If I had used my voice while I still had one, things might have turned out differently.

And now, not telling the truth had caused Otis Burdine, who always seemed to be looking for a reason to do harm, to beat on his son.

Mrs. Spangler came out of the church with Missy, and Mrs. Burdine and Jason followed, his eyebrow bandaged. Reverend Love took Jason's elbow. "I am so sorry, Jason. If I can help it, Otis won't lay a hand on you ever again. You are always welcome here. You understand me, son?"

Jason looked at him, squaring his shoulders. "I didn't steal nothing, Reverend. I didn't."

Reverend Love put his arm across Jason's shoulders. "Don't you worry, Jason. We'll get it sorted out."

They all got into the Spanglers' car, Missy and Jason in the back. Jason leaned his head against the window. I couldn't be sure if he saw me by the side of the building. He turned away, his face shadowed by the reflection of the trees on the window.

Reverend Love watched them leave, standing in the parking lot, hands on his hips.

I unglued myself from my spot. I turned, accidentally ramming my elbow into the rainspout that dangled from the roof. It fell, crumbling into several pieces, clanging onto the ground.

My hiding place discovered, Reverend Love called to me, his voice stopping me right where I stood.

"Dulcie."

He came closer, his eyes as gray as the sky, a question in them. He didn't have to say a word. I already knew what he was going to ask.

Reverend Love continued, "I need to talk to you. And Faith. You go find her, hear? Right now."

Aunt Bernie interrupted, scurrying down the church steps, apron on, dish towel in hand.

"Reverend, you best pull your car up. It's Mary."

She let out a breath, and smiled. "I think the baby's coming."

25

h-e-g-i-r-a
hegira (n.)
*a journey made for the sake of safety or an
escape; flight*

That night sleep wouldn't come, Mama. Faces floated
in front of me, the expressions on them rising in my
mind: betrayal on Jason's, desperation on Faith's, defeat on
Reverend Love's, anger on Otis Burdine's.

I couldn't think of an exact word for how I felt, Mama.
I paged through my dictionary looking for one that would
suit. "Confusion," "agitation," "upheaval." I was torn
between light things and dark things; a flood of emotions
flowed through my veins.

Finally, I settled on a word that I found in Aunt Bernie's paperback dictionary, an old *Merriam-Webster* she used
sometimes to cheat on crossword puzzles. It's what I felt.

"Remorse." *Webster's* definition: "a gnawing distress arising from a sense of guilt."

As I tossed around my in bed, voices swirled in my head: *"I didn't steal nothing, Reverend. . . . Dulcie, come on. I'd have done the same for you. . . . He would not want you to lie to protect a friend. . . . You steal from a church, you no good, worthless . . ."* I kept playing the same old records. Punching the same numbers on the jukebox.

I remembered standing on the stage in the auditorium at the state spelling bee—the day my words disappeared—the day you left. I felt the same then—full of *remorse*—for not having spoken the truth, for not changing things when I could.

But it didn't matter anymore, Mama, because I still planned on leaving Shepherdsville the next day. It was best for everybody if I packed up all the unspoken words and took them with me. I'd have to carry them around with me no matter where I went, anyway.

I went over my plan. Worked it out in my head. I'd use one of Faith's tricks. I'd ride Maybelle to the bus station in Shepherdsville, make up a story to the bus driver about how my mama was waiting on the other end with the money, then take off running when I got to Paint Creek. I'd make my way to Lilac Court, unearth the hidden key under the petunia pot, and let myself inside. I wasn't sure what would happen after that, but at least I'd be home.

Satisfied with my plan, I'd almost drifted off when the front door downstairs shook, breaking into my thoughts. Someone was pounding, rattling the windows. I looked at the clock. It was well after midnight.

Aunt Bernie's bedsprings squeaked in her room across the hall.

"What in the good Lord's name is going on?"

I turned on my light, dug my suitcase out from under the bed. I pulled out a pair of jeans, Mama, and quickly slipped them on under your Grateful Dead T-shirt. I opened the bedroom door to the hall, and found Aunt Bernie in curlers, pulling on her housecoat.

She must have been asleep for a while, because she appeared foggy, discombobulated. Taking ahold of my arm, she guided me to the top of the stairs. Together we crept down the steps, one by one, to the front door. The pounding continued, the window in the door jouncing in its frame.

"Good gravy, hold your horses," Aunt Bernie said, switching on the porch light. She parted the curtains on the window and peered out, squinting.

"It's Reverend Love," she said, sounding relieved, like she'd been expecting him for tea. But I doubted he usually made house calls this late, as a general rule.

No mind. Aunt Bernie was *always* glad to see him.

Reverend Love blew in like a stiff wind fixing to upend the furniture. He searched the room. "Is she here?" He looked at Aunt Bernie, then me. I didn't know what he was talking about.

Aunt Bernie said it for me. "Is *who* here?"

"Faith. Is she here?"

Reverend Love was still in his Sunday jacket, the seam ripped at the shoulder from his scuffle with Otis, his hair tousled, his glasses askew.

Aunt Bernie eyed me suspiciously.

I shook my head. *Why would I know where Faith is?* I hadn't seen Faith since I'd stormed away from her on the church steps.

"She's not with you?" Reverend Love ran his hands through his hair. "I've been at the hospital with Mary."

Aunt Bernie led him to a kitchen chair. "Has the baby arrived?"

Reverend Love slumped back, his legs stretched out in front of him. "No. They sent me home to get some sleep. The doctor said it might be tomorrow afternoon sometime."

"Well, goodness gracious, sakes alive." Aunt Bernie put the coffeepot on the stove and bustled around Reverend Love like a honeybee. His face drooped, slack and tired. He took off his glasses and rubbed the bridge of his nose. "I assumed she'd gotten a ride home."

He looked down at the table, shaking his head in disbelief. "I forgot about her, don't you see? In all the excitement with the baby coming, I forgot about her."

Aunt Bernie stopped midpour. "Well, you were preoccupied, for heaven's sake."

"When I got home, she wasn't there. Her bag was gone. Her guitar. Her bed wasn't slept in. I thought she'd come home with Dulcie, maybe."

Aunt Bernie remained puzzled. "Well, we haven't seen hide nor hair of her." Her eyes questioned me. "Where would she be?"

I shook my head, but I suspected I knew the answer, Mama. It was plain that Faith and me must've had the same idea. She'd just beat me to it. I figured she was long gone by now. That's all she ever talked about—leaving Shepherdsville when the time came.

Aunt Bernie sat down suddenly. "Did you check the church?"

Reverend Love wrinkled his forehead. "I stopped by on my way here. No sign of her there."

Aunt Bernie pushed a cup of coffee at him. "Where would she go? She wouldn't have made it far in the dark—all alone on these roads by herself. Surely not."

Reverend Love stared at the ceiling as if it could give him possibilities. "I searched the grounds. I walked over to Evangeline's. She helped me search the building, the basement, and the vestry."

"What about the police?"

Reverend Love ran his hand over his face. "No. I wanted to check places I thought Faith might go first. I don't want her handed over to social services. They made it clear this was her last chance. If she runs again, they'll put her in the county juvenile detention hall, then send her back to the state home."

Aunt Bernie shook her head. "Why would she take off, for heaven's sake? All of a sudden like that? She seemed settled in with you and Mary."

Reverend Love picked up the coffee cup, his hand shaking. "I should have taken more care."

"She couldn't have gone far without any money."

Reverend Love sat up, understanding everything. "I know where she got the money."

He leaned in toward me, his voice quiet. "She took the money, didn't she?"

My cheeks were on fire, my stomach turned the wrong side up.

"Dulcie, please, I'm begging you. Tell me the truth."

I didn't need to protect Faith anymore. She'd made her choice, and I couldn't do a thing about it now.

Aunt Bernie asked, "What money?"

Reverend Love explained what had happened after church service. How Jason Burdine told him Faith had stolen money from the collection plate, but then Faith had accused Jason of doing it, and that I had been called upon to settle the dispute, and had backed up Faith's story.

Aunt Bernie spoke slowly, her tongue sticking on her words. "I don't understand. Why would Faith run away if Jason stole money? Everybody knows that boy is bound for trouble, just like his daddy. Why would she . . ."

She paused, looked at me, and understood the nitty-gritty of the story. "Faith took the money?"

I nodded. *Yes, she took the money.*

"Oh, Dulcie." Reverend Love's voice was so soft, I

barely heard him. "Dulcie was trying to protect Faith." His face was so tired. "You didn't need to do that for her."

Aunt Bernie started taking her curlers out. "Let's go." She stood up and went for her pocketbook and keys on the side table.

"Reverend, you take Old Tecumseh Road out past Clifton. Check the all-night gas station by the National Road and the KOA out past the forge. Dulcie and I will head down Rebert Pike. We'll check the bus station and head out to the truck stop on Highway 70. There are only two ways out of Shepherdsville. She couldn't have gone far, unless she hitchhiked."

Reverend Love gulped a big slug of coffee and flew out the door. Aunt Bernie hustled me out to the driveway, still in her nightgown and housecoat. She called out to Reverend Love as he got into his car. "Let's meet up back at the church in ninety minutes. If we haven't found her by then, we'll try something else."

Aunt Bernie knew just want to do, like she'd done it hundreds of times before. She threw her pocketbook into the front seat, hopped in, and gunned the engine. This was a side of her I'd never seen before.

"Get in," she barked at me, like we were on an episode of that cop show, *Starsky and Hutch.*

Aunt Bernie backed out, gravel flying. She rolled down her window and shouted, "Don't worry, Reverend. We'll find her!"

I do have to say, Mama, Aunt Bernie does take charge in a crisis.

26

p-i-l-g-r-i-m-a-g-e

pilgrimage (n.)

a journey made by a pilgrim; any long journey

But we didn't find her, Mama.

Aunt Bernie and I drove to the truck stop on the highway. She leaned over the steering wheel, her face a map of consternation. We searched the country roads on the way, our headlights up bright. Aunt Bernie didn't say much as we crawled along, craning our necks forward, searching for a glimpse of Faith.

We asked at the all-night diner on Highway 70, getting plenty of stares—Aunt Bernie in her housecoat and slippers, both of us sleepy-headed and addled, our hair unbrushed and faces unwashed. Nobody we asked had seen her.

We drove the long way back to Shepherdsville to the

dinky bus station in town. It was empty, doors closed and locked. The schedule posted on the door showed that the last bus had left for Cincinnati at eight that night. If Faith had caught that bus, she surely was halfway to Nashville.

Whether it was the dark lonely roads, the bright glaring lights at the truck stop, or the night-owl people staring into their coffee at two in the morning, I realized I had been kidding myself. Mama, I wasn't cut out to take off on my own like Faith had. The true hardship of it hit me, square and true. Faith had made running seem like an adventure. I saw that night that it was plain dangerous, and nothing more. My skin crawled with fear for her.

Aunt Bernie drove us to the church. We waited for Reverend Love in the parking lot, the only light a yellow bulb left on over the church entrance, moths fluttering around it.

Leaning her head against the seat, Aunt Bernie stared out at the field ahead, her voice quiet. "I tried to find her. Tried to stop her from leaving, you know."

At first I thought she meant Faith, but I came to see she meant you, Mama.

"I looked all over. I can't remember where I was that afternoon. I came home, and our folks told me what they'd done. They'd told Emma that she couldn't live with them anymore. I thought if I found her and brought her back, they'd reconsider." She spread her fingers wide on the steering wheel.

"They never mentioned her after that. Not one word. It was as if she'd never existed. I didn't hear from her until after you were born. She sent me a letter, no address—just a postmark from some small town I'd never heard of."

Aunt Bernie rolled down her window. The night air was cool, dampening the inside of the car. I rolled my window down too, leaned my head far enough out to see stars above me.

"I worried about her, thought about her every day, but after a while I got used to her being gone. When she showed up here, after you were born, I shooed her away from the house like she was a pesky salesman. I was a coward—afraid to go against your grandfather. He was a man of faith but as hard as nails, not willing to bend an inch."

She pushed hair out of her eyes, far away in a different time.

"I've learned over the years that you get to know more about a person in their absence than you do in their presence. Influenza took both of our folks, not long after. I didn't know where to find Emma, where to look. I was so ashamed of how I'd treated her, I figured she wouldn't have let me in the door, even if I did find her."

Aunt Bernie turned to me, her eyes shiny in the dark. "In some kind of way, having you here is like having her back." She patted the seat beside me, her voice too thick to say more.

We sat in silence for a long while, watching stars beam to us from thousands of miles away, clouds moving across them in bands, making them disappear. After some time she said, "You might never see Faith again. You have to prepare for that."

I looked down at my lap and nodded. I knew that, but I didn't like to hear it.

Aunt Bernie looked up at the ceiling of the car, reached up, and fiddled with the overhead light, trying to flick it on—with no luck. "I know you were trying to protect her, but there are just some things you can't fix, you understand? No matter how much you want them to be different." She gave up her struggle with the light. She took my hand and squeezed it.

I squeezed back and continued to study the stars. Aunt Bernie was right about Faith. She might have run away in any case—telling the truth might not have changed anything for her—but I felt responsible for the whupping

Jason had gotten. The vision of Otis kicking him on the ground played over and over in my mind when I closed my eyes.

Reverend Love arrived finally, his car empty—without Faith.

He opened the church, and we helped him search the building one more time. We checked the basement and the vestry again.

Reverend Love and Aunt Bernie called out, down the hallways and in the sanctuary, "Faith. Faith!"

The empty church echoed back her name.

Reverend Love leaned against the pew nearest the doors, dark circles under his eyes. He said he needed to go back to the hospital to check on Mary. Then he walked softly beside us through the parking lot, the gravel cracking under our feet.

"Bernice, thank you." He stopped and took her hands in his. "Pray for her."

Aunt Bernie urged him into the car. "You go on now. You've a baby to shepherd into this world."

We drove back to the farm, the morning light bringing bird call. Aunt Bernie made fresh biscuits as the sun struggled to peek through an overcast Monday morning. I practically fell asleep in my gravy, I was so tired.

Aunt Bernie shooed me to bed.

I slept until lunchtime.

Later, the afternoon was gray and ominous, with thunderclouds racing across the sky. The radio announcer at WGOD issued a tornado watch, and at nightfall, rain poured as if the sky itself were boiling mad. The storm soaked the earth, leaving pools in the culverts, blowing down the clothesline. I couldn't help wondering where Faith was, hoping she was inside somewhere safe.

We got the call that Monday night that Reverend Love and his wife had had a baby girl. They named her Charity.

Still no word about Faith.

27 ⟨decorative flourish⟩

v–i–g–i–l
vigil (n.)
a purposeful or watchful staying awake during the
usual hours of sleep

Rain fell hard all Tuesday, the constant patter on the roof a reminder that Faith remained missing, maybe without shelter. I tried to read some of the books Aunt Bernie kept around—yellowed Agatha Christie and Sherlock Holmes mysteries smelling of must, none as interesting as the mystery of Faith's whereabouts.

Aunt Bernie roosted in her easy chair, knitting. A baby blanket took shape in her lap, her hands quick and nimble, needles clicking, as she watched a Billy Graham crusade televised from Cincinnati.

Something had shifted between Aunt Bernie and me since our midnight drive. We'd settled in our ways around each other, becoming cozier, peas in a pod, so to speak. I found myself seeking out Aunt Bernie's company rather than avoiding it.

We watched television together. She tried to teach me to knit. I helped her around the kitchen.

The minutes crawled; the rain fell.

No word.

By Wednesday afternoon the rain had stopped its temper tantrum and became less violent. Water continued to fall in small pellets, pinging in the hog trough and tapping the windows. Aunt Bernie had some work to do at WGOD, so she drove me over to see Evangeline at the vestry, rain pelting the windshield.

"I heard that Jason and his mother are doing fine," Aunt Bernie said. "Otis is down to the county hospital, drying out." She turned off the windshield wipers. "I thought you'd like to know."

It did make me feel better that Otis was being kept away from Jason for the time being.

When I arrived at the church vestry, Evangeline handed me the Sunday bulletin I'd placed on the shelf next to Jeremiah's sign. She said, "You left this behind."

When she turned to hunt through her sewing stuff,

I took my letter from Reverend Love's preaching robe and stuffed it into my dress pocket. Thankfully, in all the ruckus, he hadn't found it. With Faith's taking off like she had, it would have worried him even more. He would surely have told Aunt Bernie about it, who would have chained me up like old Marlow if she knew I'd considered running away.

Evangeline brought out gold thread and long embroidery needles. "I have a surprise for you. I traced the swan you drew on your Sunday bulletin and made a design from it."

Evangeline unfolded a paper pattern in the shape of a swan in flight, an exact replica of my hand-drawn picture. She pinned the pattern onto the collar of a bright lavender robe.

"We'll take gold thread and embroider the design right onto the fabric. Just follow the lines."

I threaded the needle and did my best to follow the small figure of the swan on the fabric, carefully, in and out, each stitch forging a golden path through Evangeline's pattern.

Hours passed; I barely noticed the time as I worked. Evangeline hummed quietly but didn't bring up the subject of Faith.

I wondered how Mr. Cobb and Penny Lane had fared

in the rain. I imagined the babies had grown another inch. It was far too soggy to check. Plus, I don't think Evangeline would have let me out of her sight.

When Aunt Bernie picked me up that afternoon, Evangeline pointed her finger at me, saying, "You come back tomorrow. We'll finish up. We'll want these to be ready for Baptism Sunday." She tapped the table, her palm flat. "Plus, I miss you when you're not here."

By Thursday morning the sun was shining, drying up the puddles. With the rain over, the orange tiger lilies burst out, and the oak trees in the yard shimmered, their leaves lush. I swear, Aunt Bernie's garden had grown a foot overnight. The bean plants shot up to my shoulder. Her climbing roses bloomed a crimson red next to the front porch door, their scent making the air sweet and delicate.

Aunt Bernie puttered in her garden, wearing a big moth-eaten hat. She knelt on some towels, weeding in and around her beans, while I took a spade to her lettuce patch. She sat back on her ankles, her face red, perspiration making it shine, her hair curly in the heat.

"Hard to believe that everywhere for as far as the eye can see used to belong to our family. Acres and acres of farmland, crops tended and harvested, year after year.

Here I sit, struggling with this tiny garden. Sometimes I wonder that I don't sell this place too."

She wiped her forehead with her sleeve. "But I can't let go of it. A place becomes part of you, and you carry it with you, no matter where you are."

I knew what she meant. Lilac Court was like that, and the pond behind the church.

After I finished my chores, I rode Maybelle out to the swans' nest with some biscuits from the bread box, before my afternoon's work with Evangeline.

The cygnets had sure enough grown to almost knee high, lighter feathers growing along their wings as their darker baby fuzz let loose. Penny and Mr. Cobb waited in the shallows, their necks craned, as if to say, *Where in the dickens have you been?* I tossed the biscuit bits to them, and they lazily swam to the edge, their family following. I crawled up onto the tree branch, happy to listen to their little rustles and the buzzing of the field bugs.

I had just tossed off my sneakers, Mama, when I saw something tucked in a small hollow of the tree. A tiny yellow envelope—the sort people put in the collection plate. I pulled it out. It was still damp from the rain. I turned it over and found my name written on it in pencil. I opened it, my heart jumping in my chest.

Inside was Faith's gum-wrapper bracelet, the one she'd made the day we'd visited Bean—and a twenty-dollar bill. I slipped the bracelet onto my wrist and tucked the twenty into my Bible bag. Leaving it there was clearly a sign that she meant for me to return it to Reverend Love for her.

Aunt Bernie was planning a visit to the Loves' come Saturday, when Mary returned home from the hospital. Aunt Bernie had cast on and purled like crazy, finishing up the baby blanket for Charity. That would be my chance to return the money to Reverend Love. I hoped it might ease him some, knowing that Faith had left it. Returning it was her way of saying she was sorry she'd stolen it in the first place.

That night, after Aunt Bernie had gone to bed, I dug into your old *National Geographics*, Mama, and read some of the articles about the places you'd pinned on your map. I liked knowing that you'd seen the same pictures and read the same words when you were a girl. It was a comfort, turning the same pages that you had once touched.

I read about a place called the Rock of Gibraltar in Spain, a place that sailors in olden times believed was the end of the world. They thought that if you sailed past the rock, you would fall off the end of the earth, never to be seen again.

Maybe that's where you went, Mama—both you and Faith—past the Rock of Gibraltar, or someplace like it. I found the spot on your map and traced my fingers from Ohio all the way to Spain. I pushed in a pin. I took out all the other pins and left that one. I tied a piece of yarn from Aunt Bernie's knitting basket between you and me. I put a pin in Nashville, too, and tied a piece of yarn between me and Faith and back again—a crazy-shaped star hovering over the world.

It made me think of when I was little, Mama. Remember when we'd search the sky and find the first star in the evening? We'd hook our pinkies together and wish on that star, sending our secrets up into the unknown. Sealing our wishes tight; you'd say "pins" and I'd say "needles." Then we'd blow them through our fingers, hoping they'd land where we'd sent them. We couldn't tell each other what we'd wished for, else it wouldn't come true.

That night in your room in Shepherdsville, a long while before sleep stole me away, I stared at the map and the star I'd created. A warm breeze whispered at the curtains, catching my thoughts and lifting them out and into the night, taking my wish with it.

28

a-s-c-e-n-d
ascend (n.)
to go up; move upward; rise

On Friday, while Aunt Bernie was at a Ladies' Auxiliary meeting in the church basement, I worked with Evangeline in the vestry, finishing up the new choir robes. I stitched and trimmed stray threads from hems while she embroidered the swan design on the collars. She'd taken over that task when my first two or three attempts at swans had ended up looking like flying pig ears. Her robes were a thing of beauty, Mama. Ready to wear—that is, if enough of the choir showed up to wear them on Baptism Sunday.

Evangeline had just gotten started on the very last robe, when Aunt Bernie showed up at the vestry door, looking steamed up and frazzled. Evangeline lowered her work into her lap. "Well, looky here. A visitor. We don't get many of those."

Aunt Bernie stepped in gingerly, sidestepping fabric piles. "Miss Tucker, sorry to interrupt." She extended her hand to Evangeline. "We haven't had much of a chance to talk, but I wanted to thank you for all you're doing for the church, and especially the time you've spent with Dulcie."

Evangeline took Aunt Bernie's hand. "It's my pleasure. Though I have to say, not many have expressed much interest in what we got going on in here. Have they, Dulcie?"

Aunt Bernie took a couple of steps my way and inspected my handiwork—the hem of a lemon-colored robe. "Well, my land, Dulcie. Those stitches are neat as a pin." She smiled, a nervous tic playing at her mouth. "You've taught her well."

Evangeline pooh-poohed her. "She's taught herself."

Aunt Bernie stood uncomfortably, as if spiders were crawling in her underwear. She flushed, or maybe it was the heat.

Evangeline waited.

Finally Aunt Bernie stammered, "In—in ten minutes the members of the Ladies' Auxiliary Committee are meeting with Reverend Love in the chapel."

Evangeline waited.

"They have an agenda and a petition."

Evangeline waited.

"Miss Tucker, they're going to ambush him. Good Lord, the man just had a baby, and they think now is the time to have it out about . . . well . . . about *you*."

Aunt Bernie continued. "Lavinia Swinson and the others are not happy with the changes Reverend Love has made. There's been talk about his past, and his not being a good example to his flock. His hiring you seems to be, for some of them, proof that he's not fit to lead a congregation. There's even been talk about contacting the state council." She pointed at the robes.

"They've got wind of the new choir robes, and some of them are fit to be tied about that. I know it's just an excuse, something they've latched on to . . . but . . ."

The only sound in the room was a fly that persisted in landing on Aunt Bernie's shoulder. She waved it away. I kept my head down, clipping threads.

Evangeline looked at Aunt Bernie as if Aunt Bernie had been hit upside the head and were addlepated in the extreme. "I can't change that way of thinking, Bernice."

Aunt Bernie clasped her hands together, lowered her head, and nodded. Evangeline forced a smile. "I appreciate your concerns, but there's nothing to be done about it."

"Well, I just wanted to let you know, is all. There is probably no stopping that petition, but . . . I . . . thought . . . maybe if you'd come to the meeting . . ."

Evangeline stood up, laying down the robe she was working on. "Now, Bernice, what kind of good would that do?"

Aunt Bernie looked defeated, like someone had fizzled her fireworks. "I don't know, but it seems right that you be there."

Evangeline calmly said, "I'll think about it. I will."

After Aunt Bernie left, Evangeline said, "Dulcie, you go on now. We're done for the afternoon." She walked out the vestry door without another word and out to the edge of the field. I watched through the window as Evangeline stood out there, staring at the tree line, hands on her hips.

I cleaned up, put away my scissors and thread, and hung up the robes. I headed straight for the chapel. Whatever was going to happen, I didn't want to miss it, Mama. First I'd lost you, then Ray had gone missing from my life, and then Faith had taken off for Nashville. I couldn't abide the thought of losing Evangeline, too.

I sneaked into the back of the church. There was a

good crowd of folks there to protest Evangeline's being the choir director. Aunt Bernie had settled up front with a few other ladies. I guessed they were in favor of honoring Reverend Love's choice, like Aunt Bernie, but I gathered that the majority clumped together in the middle, murmuring amongst themselves, were there to try to persuade him to find a replacement.

Of course, Mama, you can guess that Lavinia Swinson was there, fanning herself with one of the church fans on a stick, along with Mrs. Butler, Noreen Taylor with her new baby, and some other members of the Auxiliary. There were a couple of men there too, Len and Lou Young, two bachelor brothers. Their dairy farm wasn't far from Aunt Bernie's. There was rustling and whispering behind hands, everyone shifting this way and that as they waited for Reverend Love to show up. I sneaked up the side aisle to get closer, trying to keep out of sight.

Finally Reverend Love came down the steps from his office and up the center aisle to the front of the church. He wore dress pants and a white shirt, the sleeves rolled up, his fingers stained with ink. His jaw was set hard, making him resemble a boxer ready for the ring. His hair was combed and wet with Brylcreem.

He positioned himself at the front and stood below the

pulpit, before the crowd that had come there to challenge him. I swear, Mama, he took time to look each and every one of them in the eye before he spoke, settling on the leader of the pack.

"Mrs. Swinson, why don't you tell me the purpose of our gathering today?"

She stood, her pearls clacking against one another, holding a piece of paper. "I have here a petition of fifteen signatures stating that we feel a new choir director should be appointed."

Reverend Love walked up the aisle and took the paper from her. He looked it over, then turned to Mrs. Swinson, a tight smile plastered on his face.

"What I gather from this, Lavinia, is that you've managed to persuade fourteen other people to be as narrow-minded as yourself." He walked back up to the front with the petition, folded it into quarters, and stuck it into his pocket. He leaned against the raised stage of the pulpit and crossed his arms.

Mrs. Swinson was still standing. "I am not narrow-minded, Reverend. I only believe we should seek someone who has real credentials."

Reverend Love looked incredulous. "Lavinia, Shepherdsville is a small town in the middle of hundreds of acres of farmland. The nearest city is an hour away. Where would we get someone with, as you call them, credentials?"

Mrs. Swinson was prepared with her answer. "We could put an ad in the Cincinnati paper."

Reverend Love laughed. "Who do you think would move to Shepherdsville to lead a small choir for a pittance?"

Mrs. Swinson was undeterred. "Also, while I am not disputing that we could save money for a new furnace by not buying new robes, I think having a . . . a . . ."—she spat out the rest—"mish-mosh of colors will make our Sunday service no better than a Saturday cartoon. Our robes should be somber, understated. Maroon or navy—all one color."

Reverend Love looked flabbergasted. "Are you under the impression that God cares what color you wear, Lavinia?" He asked for a show of hands. "Who is in agreement with Mrs. Swinson?"

Hands shot up, some reluctantly, as Lavinia Swinson looked around at each of the others, willing them to follow her lead.

"And who is not in agreement?"

Aunt Bernie and her clutch of ladies raised their hands. I knew I wasn't counted, but I raised my hand anyway.

Reverend Love was about to speak, but he stopped, because Evangeline had come through the side door from the vestry.

Oh, how that room quieted, Mama. You could have heard even the tiniest fart.

Evangeline, looking every bit as regal as a lion, walked up the steps and across the stage past the pulpit to the organ. She calmly pulled out the bench and sat, her back as straight as a lighting rod.

Everything stopped. I held my breath.

Reverend Love took one look at Evangeline, then turned and put his hands into his pockets. He looked at the floor, the tiniest something teasing around the corners of his mouth.

Mrs. Swinson slowly sank her butt back down into the pew. No one said another word.

Evangeline held the entire church under her spell while she uncovered the keys and switched on the organ. It was quiet, the people in the pews staring at her, fascinated. I was dying to see what she was going to do.

The tension in the room rose along with the temperature, until at last Evangeline spoke. Her voice, rich and deep, bounced off the walls. It seemed to lift me off my seat, it was so powerful.

"When I was a little girl, down in Atlanta, where my people are from, I lived in a fancy house." Evangeline played a note. The organ responded with a deep tone.

"A fancy house with silver and china and fine linen imported from France. There was a baby grand piano in that house. It was one of the finest houses in all of Atlanta." Evangeline paused and played a chord.

Mrs. Swinson looked positively green, like she was going to lose her lunch.

"My mother was a maid in that house. She worked there all her life. We lived downstairs in the servants' quarters. The lady who owned that house took a liking to me." Evangeline smiled, the memory warm on her face.

"She taught me to play the piano." As if to prove it, Evangeline ran her hands over the keys of the organ, low notes to high notes, octave by octave. "But once I left that house, I didn't have a piano to play. I didn't play for a long time." Evangeline put her hands in her lap. "When I came here to Shepherdsville, I was a lost soul. My little boy had died, and I saw no reason to keep going. Reverend Moore gave me a job, and I did that job for eighteen years. I cleaned this church, every pew, every hymnal, this organ—every toilet."

All eyes were on Evangeline. No one could look away.

I gripped the edge of the pew, squeezing the wood with all my might.

"For eighteen years, when there was no one here but me, I'd come to this very organ and I'd play." Evangeline touched the organ tenderly. "I played music for my little boy. All the songs he didn't ever get to hear. I played and I played and I played. And it saved me." Evangeline played one final note. "Saved me."

No one moved or spoke. I noticed that Mrs. Taylor, who was holding her sleeping baby, appeared to be close to busting into tears.

Evangeline said softly, "If you would, please open a hymnal." There was a moment of incomprehension.

Reverend Love quietly told them, "Go on, y'all." Everyone did as he said, taking the hymnals out of their places in the backs of the pews, rustling them open.

"If you would be so kind as to call out a hymn number," Evangeline said.

There was a moment of silence. It was Aunt Bernie who spoke first. "Hymn number 391."

Evangeline didn't have a hymnal, or music in front of her at all. She knew what Hymn 391 was without looking.

"O Happy Day That Fixed My Choice."

Then she played and sang it. All the verses. Oh,

Mama, Evangeline made the woodwork vibrate and the windows shake, her singing a thing of glory, as pure as pure. A person couldn't hear her voice and not have their heart rise up to meet it.

> *Happy day, happy day,*
> *When Jesus washed my sins away!*
> *He taught me how to watch and pray,*
> *And live rejoicing every day*

Someone else called out a number after Evangeline hit the last notes.

"Hymn 214."

Evangeline knew that one too.

"The Old Rugged Cross." She was just getting warmed up, apparently.

> *So I'll cherish the old rugged cross,*
> *Till my trophies at last I lay down;*
> *I will cling to the old rugged cross,*
> *And exchange it some day for a crown.*

Everybody kept calling numbers, and Evangeline kept playing those hymns, Mama. It was clear she knew every hymn in the book, every single verse, every single word.

Evangeline was *magnificent*.

"Magnificent." *Webster's* definition: "beautiful in a grand or stately way; exceptionally good." I only wished Faith had been there to see it.

It wasn't long before people started singing along, especially those who were choir members. There was clapping and swaying, and everyone forgot the reason they were there in the first place—which was to get rid of Evangeline.

At last Reverend Love held up his hand. Everyone quieted and listened. "When I first came to Redeemer, I was alone in my office one day. Evangeline Tucker didn't know I was in the building. I overheard her playing music, singing like the angels themselves. I thought her talents were going to waste, cleaning this building, so I offered her the job of choir director."

He looked right at Lavinia Swinson and said, "Her credentials were clear to me, and I hope now to you, too. Are there any more questions?"

Mrs. Swinson blurted, "Well, but who is cleaning the church, then?"

Reverend Love smiled. "The members of the Youth Bible Study Group have been helping out now and again, when they need a change of pace. But we haven't had an official cleaning person since I began. I was thinking the Ladies' Auxiliary could form a committee and circulate the duties amongst y'all. That would be a big help to this congregation, wouldn't it, Lavinia? Could you manage it?"

Mrs. Swinson looked like someone had stuck a sock right in her mouth.

Reverend Love continued, "Now, it is true that new choir robes are being made for services. The old ones were worn to threads. I hope you'll agree that the new ones will be a welcome addition. Having all one color, like it was before—well, I understand it's what you're used to, but I like Evangeline's idea. I hope the new robes will brighten services and help us appreciate the many colors the Lord put on this earth."

Reverend Love smiled. "May I please see a show of hands of those in favor of Evangeline Tucker's continued placement as choir director and approval of the new robes?"

Everyone's hand went up, Mama. Every single person's. Mrs. Swinson's was the last, but after looking around her at all the hands in the air, she realized she was defeated.

Afterward folks rose in a hubbub, clearly impressed.

Some hurried out to their cars, like Lavinia Swinson, but many went up to speak to Evangeline.

I watched Reverend Love. He took the folded petition out of his pocket, balled it up, and arched it through the air to the metal trash can in the hallway, outside the sanctuary door.

It was a prayer shot for sure, but he made it—a perfect swish.

29

r-e-j-o-i-c-e
rejoice (v.)
to be glad, happy, or delighted; be full of joy

When I looked down at Charity in her Moses basket, her face puckered up like a buttercup, I'd had no idea how delicate babies were, Mama. Her tiny nails and wispy hair reminded me of the cygnets—awkward and elegant at the same time.

Aunt Bernie had made a plate of sugar cookies with pink icing, and we'd brought them over to the Loves' house Saturday afternoon, along with the soft pastel-colored knitted blanket for the baby. I had the twenty-dollar bill in my pocket, still tucked in its envelope. When the time was right, I aimed to give it to Reverend Love.

We'd picked up Evangeline on our way over to the Loves'. She'd brought a teeny tiny rose-colored choir robe she'd made for Charity. Aunt Bernie oohed and aahed over it, but I could tell she was miffed that Evangeline had outdone her in the giving department. Evangeline knew just what to do, though. She oohed and aahed over Aunt Bernie's baking talent.

"Bernice Dixon, you ought to have a bake shop. Those cookies smell like heaven."

Aunt Bernie beamed.

The Loves' kitchen counter was blanketed with food in containers and on fancy plates. Apparently, having a baby is an excuse for a bonanza of food.

Aunt Bernie sat next to me on the sofa. Evangeline and Reverend Love relaxed on the piano bench and talked about the baptism service the Sunday after next.

"You want to hold her?" Mary asked me. I didn't know that I wanted to, until I did. Mary gently positioned Charity in my lap, the baby's head resting on my arm. "I'll bring out a plate for y'all. We've more than we know what to do with."

Aunt Bernie's hard places softened around Charity. Her face was tender as she watched the baby sleep in my arms. "I held you when you were a baby. Did you know that?"

I gave Aunt Bernie all my attention.

"When your mother showed up at the door of the farm, I told her she'd better go. She begged me to meet her, down at the Old Mill. I made some excuse to our folks and met her there."

This was news to me. Mama, why didn't you ever tell me?

Aunt Bernie ran her finger along Charity's cheek. "You were such a little thing, just like Charity. Your mama loved you so much. No matter what she'd been through, you were the center of her universe, that was clear. I held you for a while, and you looked right at me, your eyes like little pieces of blue sky—wise, even then." She sighed. "Emma had hoped that if our folks saw you, they'd change their minds and let the two of you stay. I told her not to expect that. When I explained that they never even spoke of her, Emma understood it was no use, and left town."

She put her finger into Charity's grasp and whispered in the baby's direction. "I should have gone with her. I know that now." Aunt Bernie flushed, her voice thick and overcome with emotion. She took a drink of lemonade and cleared her throat. "Mary, can I help with those cookies?"

Reverend Love sank into the sofa next to me, his face clean-shaven, nicked on the chin. He looked even younger than usual. I couldn't believe he was somebody's daddy now.

"It's a miracle, isn't it? A brand-new soul. Pure. Come Baptism Sunday, in the Lord's eyes your soul will be as pure as hers."

What a crazy thing, Mama, that Reverend Love and all of them believed that taking a bath in front of people would wash away all of it—the weight of all of those things too heavy to float. Hitting Loretta. Getting Jason in trouble. Not telling the truth about Faith. Leaving you.

Reverend Love took the baby from me. I wrapped my fingers around the envelope in my pocket, waiting for the time to hand it over and let him know where I'd found it, giving away my secret about the swan's nest. I had my smiley-face notebook in my Bible bag, and was ready to write out what I needed to say. But I was afraid, Mama, that if I told, I wouldn't be able to visit Penny and Mr. Cobb anymore.

A knock sounded at the door. Reverend Love got up to answer.

Through the screen I could see an Ohio state highway patrolman standing on the porch, his shiny badge glistening in the sunlight.

"Reverend Love?"

Mary came out of the kitchen, alarm on her face, a plate of brownies and cookies in her hands. She dropped it onto the coffee table with a plunk and held out her hands to take Charity from Reverend Love. His voice was soft, fearful. "How can I help you, officer?"

The patrolman peered inside at all of us. "Sir, could you step outside, please?"

Mary put her hand on Reverend Love's shoulder. "Anything you have to say, you can say in front of me." She handed the baby to Evangeline.

Aunt Bernie and I got up from the sofa. Reverend Love and Mary followed the patrolman outside. We gathered around the screen door, practically pressing our noses against it. The highway patrol cruiser was parked in the driveway behind Aunt Bernie's car.

"Please wait there, sir," the officer said.

Reverend Love and Mary stood in the yard, holding tight. Everything moved in slow motion. It took the patrolman an eternity to reach the back door of his vehicle and open it.

Faith stepped out from the car. Her body seemed smaller than I remembered. She had dark circles under her eyes. Her hair was greasy, her clothes wrinkled.

I shot out the door and onto the porch, like a bullet.

The patrolman led Faith forward. "We picked this gal up in Centerville, hitchhiking. She's lucky nobody took it into their heads to pick her up. She said she belongs here. Gave this address. Wouldn't give me her name."

Faith stood by the patrolman, her eyes round.

Reverend Love stood, as rooted as a tree, her name falling off his lips. "Faith."

"S'cuse me, sir. What did you say?"

"Faith. Her name is Faith."

I grabbed ahold of the porch post, hoping he wouldn't send her away. But it was Mary who stepped forward. "She does. Belong here." She looked at Reverend Love. "With us."

Reverend Love took a few steps until he was in front of Faith. "Yes, we had a bit of a misunderstanding. But that's all over now. Isn't it?"

Faith nodded and walked straight into his arms.

Reverend Love held her tight, then sent her into Mary's waiting arms. He said to the patrolman, "Sorry for your trouble. We'll keep a better eye on her. Y'all don't need to worry about that."

Mary gave Faith a good looking-over, cupping her face gently. "Let's get you inside. Nothing a bath won't cure."

Reverend Love walked the patrolman to his vehicle. Faith crossed the yard with Mary.

When they got to the porch, Faith stopped in front of me. She didn't have to say anything. Her face said it all.

I pulled the yellow envelope out of my pocket and passed it to her. She took it.

"I'll give it to him. Thanks for hanging on to it for me."

Faith touched the gum-wrapper bracelet on my wrist. I pulled it off and offered it back. She stopped me. A smile broke across her dirt-streaked face. "No, I wanted you to have it. You know, like a friendship bracelet."

I slipped it back on, so that it was circling my wrist, more precious than diamonds.

Mary put her arms around us. "Come on inside, girls. Faith, there is someone I'd like you to meet."

30

g-r-a-t-i-t-u-d-e
gratitude (n.)
warm, appreciative response to kindness; thankfulness

While Evangeline fitted my baptism gown, Faith held the pins. Evangeline picked up the ends of the fabric, fashioning a hem around the bottom.

"You look like you belong on the top of a Christmas tree." Faith laughed. "Are you sure you're going through with this?"

I looked at myself in the mirror. I didn't have a choice. Reverend Love and, especially, Aunt Bernie had their hearts set on it.

Evangeline said, "You'll want to bring an extra set of drawers."

Faith spewed the Coke she was drinking all over her

shirt. "'Drawers'?" We collapsed in a heap, giggling. "You mean underwear?"

Evangeline rolled her eyes. "Lordy be."

I took off the gown, and Evangeline shooed us out of the vestry. We sat on the picnic tables waiting for Reverend Love to give me instructions on how to get baptized. Baptism Sunday was in two days.

Faith picked some dandelions by the side of the parking lot, then sat braiding them together. She didn't look at me while she worked. It had been almost a week since she'd come back.

I was surprised when she spoke, the words rushing out fast, like she couldn't control them.

"What I did was so stupid, Dulcie. Mostly because I realized you were a good friend. You stood up for me when I didn't deserve it. I left you in a tight spot."

She concentrated hard on her chain, her fingers working the stems back and forth.

"I talked myself into believing that it didn't matter. I had it in my head that I was going to leave here anyway. It wasn't until you walked away from me that night that I realized I did care. I didn't want to leave here. I wanted to stay. But I got scared."

The mound of dandelions beside her shrank as she added them to her creation.

"I went out to the swan's nest to think. When I came back to the church, everybody was gone. Evangeline wasn't at the old minister's house. I walked all the way back to the Loves' house, but they weren't home either. I planned on telling the truth to Preach, but the whole world had gone missing. I got to feeling so bad, I packed my stuff and took off. I convinced myself that nobody cared, 'cause of what I'd done."

Faith braided the stems, her fingers stained buttery-gold. She rubbed her nose, and it left a mark.

"I didn't know that Charity was being born and that Otis Burdine had gone wild on Jason. I was too ashamed of myself to come out to your farm. I told myself I was quits with Shepherdsville, that I didn't belong here. But the whole time, a part of me knew that this is right where I belonged."

She finished her work and placed the crown of dandelions on my head. "I didn't get very far, anyway. I sneaked into the KOA and found a rental cabin nobody was using, and slept there. I took what I needed from campsites—hot dogs and stuff to eat—until the manager caught me and called the cops. I hid in a ditch and had started hitching back when the highway patrolman found me."

Reverend Love poked his head out of the vestry door. "Dulcie, you ready?"

The sanctuary was cool when we entered, though sunlight streamed through the windows in long beams. Reverend Love took this whole baptism thing real serious, Mama.

"Now, first of all, you'll wait out on the galilee." I didn't know what he was talking about. He smiled. "That's church-speak for 'porch.' After my sermon Mrs. Wheeler will play 'All Things Bright and Beautiful' on the organ. Evangeline will cue the choir, and you'll go change. When you have on your robe, you go out the vestry door and back around to the front. You'll wait there during the collection. Then, when you hear the processional, you'll come down the aisle." He walked up the steps to the altar. "To me, up here."

Reverend Love wheeled out a big square box as high as his waist. A golden cross was etched on it. It was the weirdest contraption I'd ever seen, Mama. The top flipped back to reveal porcelain inside, like a tiny tub, except it didn't have water in it yet. Steps folded down for a person to climb up to the edge.

"I'll lead you up the steps, and you'll turn around with your back to the inside of the baptismal pool."

There was a small seat that tilted backward inside the tub. "I'll stand over here. You'll sit. I'll say the prayer. You hold your nose, and I'll dip you back. I'll hold on to you. You'll only be under for a few seconds."

Faith looked skeptical. "What about her feet and legs? Won't she be only half baptized?"

Reverend Love gave Faith a stop-kidding-around look. "It's not necessary to get entirely wet."

"Who thought this stuff up, anyway?" Faith asked.

"It's been around since Biblical times. What's important is the purpose. It's for personal salvation. The water represents purification."

Faith screwed up her face, confused. "I thought this was for babies."

"It can be. But it's for anyone, at anytime, whoever needs it or wants it."

Faith looked at me. "But what if she doesn't want to be baptized?"

"Then she doesn't have to." Reverend Love looked at me. "You have to believe, in order for it to work."

Faith peered inside the pool.

"So, it's possible that if she doesn't believe in it, it's

not going to do a darn thing except get her all wet on a Sunday morning?"

Reverend Love smiled at me. "Could be. But that's a chance Dulcie is going to have to take."

I sat in the seat and wondered. I didn't see how being dunked in that contraption would wash away all of the things that had become a part of me. Nothing could take away the fact that the world is full of people who find reasons to turn their own daughter away, or the fact that running away from home makes sense sometimes. Nothing could change a world where people hurt their kids, or alter it enough so that you don't suffer the loss of the ones you love, or make it so that people don't sometimes feel bad enough to want to stop living, and take the only way out.

No, Mama, the world didn't make sense. All those things couldn't just be washed away, could they? It seemed mighty probable that all I was going to get was wet on a Sunday morning.

31

d-o-g-m-a

dogma (n.)

an opinion; that which one believes

In the vestry that Sunday morning, the gauzy white gown Evangeline had fitted for me hung on its hanger, waiting. Once I went through the sanctuary doors, Mama, I'd have to go through with it—washing everything away like dirt down the drain. The slate wiped clean.

Aunt Bernie had knocked herself out with flower arrangements. White, purple, and yellow blossoms popped out of baskets near the altar. Reverend Love wore a special white robe on top of his regular church clothes. Evangeline and the choir were decked out in the new rainbow-colored robes, and I had to admit, they were an eyeful. Redeemer practically gleamed with brightness.

Before the service, I overheard Mrs. Swinson say to

Mrs. Spangler about the new robes, "Did you ever think you'd see anything like those in the house of the Lord?"

Mrs. Spangler shook her head and harrumphed loudly.

When her mother wasn't looking, Loretta smirked at Faith and me. Faith made a gesture in reply that shouldn't be made in church.

Faith dragged me over to Jason and his mother in the parking lot when they arrived. Jason's face flashed red when he saw us. Faith was fearless.

"Jason. No hard feelings, okay? I apologize for what I did. Don't blame Dulcie. It wasn't her fault. I put her up to it." I had a feeling her apology was something Reverend Love had put *her* up to.

Jason's eyes were cold. Faith stuck out her hand. "Do unto others and all that, you know. I'm sorry. I really am. Dulcie is too."

I agreed with all my heart. I tried to let him see that it couldn't be truer.

Jason ignored her hand.

Mrs. Burdine said, "Jason appreciates that. Don't you, Jason?" She nudged him.

"Yeah, whatever."

Jason pushed past us and opened the back of the Burdines' truck, led Marlow out, and tied him to the truck door. Otis wasn't with them, still off taking the cure, I supposed.

We took our seats inside, and finally, after the longest sermon in the history of the world, Mrs. Wheeler began the hymn that was my signal to change into my robe.

The choir rose together, a living, breathing rainbow, each shiny robe like a piece of a human kaleidoscope. A golden embroidered swan glittered on every collar. Evangeline stood out in front in a royal purple gown and a multicolored silk scarf to lead the largest choir assembly I'd ever seen on a Sunday. It seemed there were more people in the choir than in the pews.

Faith squeezed my hand. She whispered, "Don't drown," and gave me a wicked smile.

In the vestry I put on my baptism robe. I checked out my gown in the cracked mirror, making sure my slip covered all the right parts, not recognizing the girl I saw there. I looked like an anxious bride-to-be, ready to run.

I could hear Reverend Love speaking in the chapel to the congregation, his voice echoing in waves, rising and lowering. I just wanted the whole thing to be over with, Mama.

When the organ sounded, I left the vestry and went outside to the front of the church.

As I stood before the church doors, the gauzy white sleeves of the gown fell over my hands like angel wings. The sun beat down on my back as I waited for the processional.

Out of the corner of my eye, I saw something move.

Marlow.

Head to the ground, his lean tail wagging, he searched willy-nilly around the picnic tables. Part of his leash dragged along behind him. He'd either come untied or had yanked himself free. Roaming where his nose led him, he headed out to the field, sniffing the ground.

I patted my leg, trying to get him to come to me. He ignored me, snorting along the edge of the field. I snapped my fingers to get his attention. Marlow turned his head and looked at me, with no intention of stopping his romp. He galloped through the patchy field, his brown coat barely visible as he loped through the grasses.

I clapped and blew air through my fingers, trying to whistle. By the time I reached the edge of the field, he was on the path alongside the fence line, headed straight for the broken fence and the NO TRESPASSING sign.

My heart shot straight into my feet. Marlow was a hunting dog—a bird dog—trained to smell out birds. I took off running as fast as the crazy gown would allow. I picked up the hem, threw it over my arm, and pumped my legs, determined to catch Marlow before he went over the fence.

He jumped over the broken part of the fence easily. That old dog was spryer than he had any reason to be, Mama. Happy to be running wild, free of his chain, he bounded like a pup.

As I clumsily made my way over the fence, the sleeve of my gown snagged on the same nail I'd caught the very first time I'd gone over, which slowed me down. I had to unhook myself.

Marlow barked, his excited yaps confirming that he'd found the swans. My side ached and pinched. My lungs heaved. It felt like heavy boots were stomping on my chest. My breath came in ragged waves, my stomach threatening to upend itself entirely.

When I got to the edge of the water, I spied Marlow, intent on the swans, searching for a way to get to them through the thick sedge grass at the water's edge. Mr. Cobb circled the cygnets in alarm. He and the babies plopped into the water, aiming for the far side of the pond. Penny stood on the nest on the small island in the middle, her wingspan extended fully. She hissed and flapped in fury at Marlow.

Marlow found his way along the upended oak tree,

inching his way along the trunk to Penny and the nest. The tree was wide enough to hold him, and though he almost lost his balance, his nails dug in.

I stood at the pond's edge, Mama, gasping and fighting for air. I picked up a stick and threw it at Marlow, hoping to stop him from his intent. My arm was rubbery and weak. The branch landed in the water and stuck in the reeds.

Everything sped up, like a movie in fast-forward.

Penny flew at Marlow. Her wings pounded and struck him, but he was trained to go for her weak spots. Mr. Cobb, only a few yards away, on the other side, flapped his wings in sympathy and concern, hissing and hovering over the cygnets.

Penny hit Marlow in the side, punching him with one of her powerful wings. He yelped. She pecked at his snout, jabbing him hard. Marlow became infuriated. He growled and jumped at her. She beat her wings frantically, stirring up leaves and dirt, backing away.

With one last giant lunge, Marlow dove at Penny. His teeth settled around her long neck. She flailed back and forth in agony. Bright blood spilled down onto her white feathers, her wings continuing to beat despite her injury.

I stumbled closer to the edge of the pond and waded in—hoping to help Penny. The air from her wings whooshed past my face. I grunted—sounds from my throat, raw and desperate, as I tried to make my way to her.

Marlow shook her back and forth. Unable to defend herself any longer, Penny became limp in his teeth. In distress Mr. Cobb hustled the babies out of the water on the far side of the pond, ruffling his feathers, hissing in fury. He had saved the babies but couldn't help Penny. Neither could I.

Penny made noises—horrible ones, like air escaping out of a balloon. I was knee-deep in the water, the gown pulling like dead weight around my feet.

Marlow shook Penny until she lay still, blood flowing from her wound, her beautiful long neck crumpled in the leaves of the nest.

Then, Mama, a place deep inside me exploded. The force of it was hot and thick, like lava.

I heard a strange sound. So loud that I covered my ears. It took me some time to realize it was me—screaming, "No. No. No. No," over and over, my voice rising above the nest—escaping as if it, too, were a bird in flight.

32

b-a-p-t-i-s-m

baptism (n.)

any experience or ordeal that initiates, tests,
or purifies

Once my voice came out of me, Mama, I couldn't seem to stop hollering.

"NO, Marlow! Noooo! Get away!" I screamed.

Marlow sniffed at Penny, his tail wagging uncertainly.

I pushed toward the nest, but the baptism gown was waterlogged and heavy. In the middle of the pond, swollen with the recent rains, the water was up to my chest. My feet and ankles became twisted up in the fabric and entwined in tendrils of undergrowth. I couldn't move.

Marlow's attention was drawn to the babies on the other side. He splashed into the water and dog-paddled toward them. My voice cracked as it screeched out of me.

"No, Marlow! No. Stop. Come back."

The gown seemed to have a life of its own, pulling me under. I was stuck in place and couldn't swim. I kicked hard and got one foot free of the fabric, but the muck underneath me gave way and sucked me down. I flopped my arms in an attempt to stay above the water, but after squirming around in the heavy baptism gown, the strength drained right out of me.

I poked my head up high enough to squeal, "Help!" as loudly as I could.

Nasty brackish water went down my throat. I swallowed it, choking, kicking my legs furiously, aiming for the shore, willing myself to move. I tore at my robe, making an effort to take it off.

"Help." My voice rasped out of my throat, hoarse and gravelly.

Marlow had reached the other side. Mr. Cobb stood his ground in front of the dog before him, wings extended, preparing to defend himself and protect the babies. The cygnets darted here and there, frantic, afraid to leave Mr. Cobb's side.

I went under again. I was so tired, Mama.

So tired.

All of a sudden I felt peaceful. I didn't want to fight

anymore. My arms and legs went limp, and I let myself float underwater. I felt like I'd been transported into a quiet dream world, lit with sunlight sparkles.

It was then that you came to me, Mama. It was as real as could be. Your voice right in my ear. "Dulcie."

Your face came into view. It was such a relief to see you, Mama. All I wanted to do was go to you. I could have reached out and taken your hand, you were so close.

But you shook your head. "Fight, Dulcie. Don't you dare give up. Keep kicking. Rise on up."

But I resisted, floating, letting the dark come in.

Your voice became urgent. "Dulcie, come on, baby. Kick."

I scissor-kicked my legs, pushing my head up, choking on bits of leaves and water weeds.

Everything got confused after that. A sound filled the world, so enormous, I couldn't locate the direction of it. It echoed in the trees all around me.

A gunshot.

Hands grabbed my shoulders, my waist—someone was behind me, pulling and dragging me out of there.

I blinked, trying to see through the guck in my eyes. Jason Burdine stood at the foot of the weeping willow, hunting rifle to his eye. In a daze I watched as he aimed and fired again.

Jason shot Marlow just as he reached Mr. Cobb.

Faith's voice echoed in my head. A wild scream that was my name.

Strong hands lifted me up and out of the water. I coughed, my eyes and ears filled with liquid, my body covered in thick muck.

Someone picked me up and carried me. I squinted, trying hard to see. Reverend Love had me in his arms. He stumbled through the muddy water and lifted me up onto solid ground, my weight sinking him to his knees. His glasses slid askew, his face intent.

"Let's get you out of here."

He stood, lifted me again, and carried me beyond the fence, through the field, to the back of the church, Faith following along. "Is she all right? Is she?"

My eyes blurry, I could make out folks huddled in groups near the picnic tables, their faces a sea of concern. Evangeline stood near the vestry door, her hand over her heart. She met us, then walked alongside Reverend Love as he brought me inside. "Lord have mercy."

He settled me into Evangeline's old stuffed chair.

I turned my head and coughed up brown goo.

Suddenly Aunt Bernie was beside me. Her frightened eyes told me everything I needed to know. I shivered, my body covered in goose bumps—those goose bumps a sure sign that her love was a real thing, Mama. True-blue.

Sobs racked me, my chest heaving. I coughed and cried, trying to tell her what I'd wanted to say for so long.

"I couldn't save her. I couldn't . . ."

Aunt Bernie stroked my face, cradling my head.

"I know, sweet girl, I know."

33

b-l-e-s-s-i-n-g
blessing (n.)
a grace said before or after eating; the gift of divine favor; good wishes or approval; anything that gives happiness or prevents misfortune

Following doctor's orders, Aunt Bernie kept me in bed for a few days. I'd swallowed a good deal of mucky water and had a nasty cough. Despite my raspy throat, I couldn't stop talking. A flood of words kept coming as if somebody had turned on the faucet and removed the handles—just pouring out of me, Mama.

"Aunt Bernie, this is really good chicken soup, best soup I ever had. I think it's making me better. . . . I really do feel fine. . . . I think I can get out of bed today. . . . I don't have a fever. . . . My cough is almost gone. . . . I need to get up to check on Mr. Cobb and the babies. . . . I have stuff to do. . . . I was thinking . . ."

She interrupted me. "Pipe down, Dulcie. Rest. Plenty of time for all that."

I tried to sit up, feeling woozy but determined not to show it. I thought if I flattered her, she'd give in.

"No, the soup is like magic. Really. Every sip is restoring me to health. How do you make it? Is there a secret recipe or something? It's not like anything I've ever had before."

Aunt Bernie sat on the end of the bed. "That's because it doesn't come from a can. I thought I'd never say this, but be quiet now. Rest."

Faith visited me, as soon as Aunt Bernie said it was okay. One of the first things I asked her was how she managed to get Reverend Love and Jason to the swan's nest.

"After they played your entrance music and you didn't show up, Preach was fixin' to blow a gasket. He gave me the eye, and I went to look for you, to see what was holding you up. I figured you'd decided not to go through with it."

She pulled a stick of gum out of her pocket, popped it into her mouth, and handed me a piece.

"Where'd you get that from?" I asked.

"From Bean. And no, I didn't steal it." She smirked. "Anyway, like I was saying, on Baptism Sunday when I went outside, you weren't on the porch. I searched the parking lot and the cemetery. When I didn't find you, I figured that you'd gone to the swans' nest. Then I heard yelling and Marlow barking out behind the church, and I put two and two together."

She put her feet up on my bed. "Later, Preach told me he had known something was wrong. He just figured you'd chickened out so he had gone ahead and finished the service. Anyway, as people came out the door of the church, I searched for Jason, figuring he'd want to know his dog was on the loose. When I found him, I told him I suspected his dog had hopped the fence and was rousting the swans back behind the church. He raced to the Burdines' truck and grabbed his daddy's hunting rifle from the back window. I shouted after him, 'What the devil do you need that thing for?' He told me Marlow was a hunting dog, and didn't I get what would happen to those birds? He said he had to stop Marlow. I told him to follow me, and we took off running. Preach saw us from the porch and came after us. He yelled, 'Where in heaven's name are y'all going with a gun?'"

She did a real good Reverend Love imitation.

"I told him you were at the nest and that Marlow was

after the swans. He hollered, 'Show me where she is,' and before I could say another word, we heard you yelling. Preach took off running, hellbent for leather."

I leaned back on the pillows. "You saved my life."

Faith met my eyes, then looked down. She plucked at stray threads of the crocheted afghan at my feet. "Well, maybe you saved mine, too."

I changed the subject before we got all sappy.

"I feel bad about Marlow."

"Yeah, me too. Marlow was just doing what he'd been taught to do. It's a hunting dog's job to flush out birds—pheasants and such. Jason said Marlow had never had a bird fight back at him like that. Marlow's instincts kicked in, and he did what came naturally. Preach told me that Jason didn't have much choice though, once Marlow had injured Penny. Marlow was trained to sit when he heard a gunshot. But when Jason fired his gun to get Marlow's attention, Marlow just kept at those birds. He might have done in the rest of the swans, if Jason hadn't stopped him. Bean said the sheriff would have had to put the dog down in any case, for killing a swan. It's the law. Jason knew Marlow didn't have a chance either way. He figured he'd rather be the one to do it."

Faith and I were silent for a moment. "Bean said they

could bury Marlow there. They made a nice spot for him," she said.

"Bean?"

"Oh, where you were trespassing? That's Bean's land."

I coughed. "What?"

"Yeah, that's his land. Been in his family forever. The sheriff made him fix the fence, after what happened."

"What about the swans? How are they doing?"

"I went out there with Evangeline. Bean and them buried Penny. Poor Mr. Cobb just stayed put on the other side of the pond, watching. I think he's a little lost without her, but the babies seemed okay. Evangeline said not to worry, the mama taught them well, and they'll do just fine. Soon as you get well, we'll go see them. Bean said it would be all right."

Aunt Bernie came in. "Faith, you go on and let Dulcie sleep."

Faith hopped off the bed. "Sure thing, Miss Bernie. I gotta get back anyway. I promised I'd help Mary give Charity a bath this afternoon."

"I'm sure you'll be a good big sister to her."

Faith smiled her lopsided smile. "Yeah, I'm going to try to be."

Aunt Bernie stopped Faith at the door of my room.

"It's an important job, you know." Faith nodded solemnly, then escaped down the stairs.

After a couple of days, Aunt Bernie let me go to the couch in the living room to watch TV, and she allowed me to have more visitors. People stopped by in a steady stream.

Everybody brought food until the kitchen was overflowing with casseroles, Jell-O molds, cookies, and brownies. One thing they know how to do in Shepherdsville is eat, Mama.

Even the Swinsons brought something over.

A pie.

Aunt Bernie held it up after they left and said, "What do you think?"

I shook my head and hooted, "No way."

She dumped it into the trash. "Agreed."

Reverend Love came to see me. I told him I was mighty sorry to have botched the whole baptism thing. He said he figured I'd already been baptized in a fashion and not to worry about that.

"I am sure you've heard it before, but I'll say it anyway. The Lord . . ."

I finished it for him, "Works in mysterious ways."

He took something out of his pocket and handed it to me. It was a small book.

"I thought you might like this. It's my favorite."

I read the cover. "William Blake."

I opened a page and read the words aloud: "'I heard an Angel singing / When the day was springing . . .'"

Reverend Love, speaking softly, finished it, "'Mercy, Pity, Peace / Is the world's release.'"

I thanked him for the book and asked after the Youth Bible Study Group.

"We've disbanded for the rest of the summer, due to lack of interest. In any case, it's almost harvest time, and school's coming up. Next summer Evangeline is fixing to lead a youth choir instead, so I'll have more time with Charity. Maybe you'll consider joining them."

I laughed and told him, "Reverend Love, I do have my voice back, but when Evangeline hears me sing, I'm sure she'll put me in charge of organizing sheet music or something."

"That bad?"

"That bad."

"You're in good company, then, 'cause I can't sing a lick myself."

. . .

Evangeline brought me a small box, a sewing kit of my very own, with everything I'd need to learn to embroider. She set me up with a simple design—a forget-me-not— and sat with me while I finished it, teaching me the knots. We didn't talk much.

That's one of the things I love about Evangeline. Words aren't needed.

When she got up to leave, I grabbed her hand.

"Evangeline, thanks for teaching me . . ." I didn't mean the sewing and embroidery, Mama, but for showing me what having a voice really means.

Evangeline didn't say anything, just squeezed my hand.

And, Mama, you'll never guess who else came over.

Jason Burdine.

His mother brought over a casserole to Aunt Bernie and pushed Jason in my direction. He leaned against the archway in the living room, shy and red-faced, his hair falling over his eyes.

"Glad you're feeling better."

Jason and I were probably the least likely of people to be friends, but something had shifted, and in that shift we'd become, not friends exactly, but less apt to fuss. I appreciated his showing up, anyway.

"I'm really sorry about Marlow," I said. "He was a good dog."

Jason looked at the rug. "Yeah, he was. He didn't mean to cause no harm. It's just what he was trained for, to roust out birds. When the swan went at him, Marlow just fought back." Then Jason said, real quietly, "I had to stop him from going after them swans. He didn't know no better."

"I know," I said.

I told him I was real sorry for all the trouble I'd caused him with Reverend Love.

He shoved his hands into his pockets. "I was a real jerk before, teasing and all that. I don't blame you, for sticking it to me."

There was an uncomfortable silence.

"Well, thanks for stopping to see me . . ."

"Hey," he said suddenly. "Want to see my new dog?"

I followed him out to their truck, Aunt Bernie calling after me to take it easy the whole way. Jason brought out a chocolate-brown pup, all long legs and tongue.

"I call him McCartney."

"McCartney?" I laughed. "Funny name for a dog."

"Faith told me that the swan Marlow killed, you'd named her Penny Lane, like the Beatles song? Well, Paul

McCartney wrote that song. So I thought my new dog's name should be . . ."

"McCartney."

"My dad brought him by when he heard about Marlow. My mom won't let my dad back into the house, for now. I guess giving me the dog is his way of trying to make up for . . . well . . . anyway."

I could tell from Jason's face, Mama, that a new dog wasn't going to make up for a darn thing that Jason had gone through. But I thought it was pretty brave of him to try to move on, in spite of it.

Jason and I played with McCartney in the grass for a little while, until Aunt Bernie called me back in, all in a dither about me being on my feet too long. Jason asked the funniest thing before I went inside. "I was thinking of asking Faith to go to the movies sometime. Do you think she'd go?"

I smiled, his being sweet on her tickling me something crazy. "Yeah, I think she might."

He blew out a puff of air, relief in it. "Cool."

Ray showed up too, Mama.

We sat on the back porch, him in a busted-out wicker chair and me on the old swing. The crops in the fields towered around us, a sea of green swaying as far as we could see. Ray clearly had something on his mind but had trouble getting started. He stuck his boot out in front of him and twirled one ankle, then the other. Years of trucking left him doing the oddest things to unglue his muscles.

Ray swung his chair around to me, his eyes clear, the crevices in his cheeks deep architecture carved and designed for his face alone. He studied his boot tips, rubbing his face. Then he spoke, his voice cracking. "If something ever happened to you . . . well, I wouldn't be worth a fig ever after. You aren't my blood, but I care for you as if you were my own. Your mama meant the world, but now that she's gone, I want to do my best by you. That's why I brought you here in the first place."

I gripped the chain of the porch swing.

"I know, Ray."

He coughed, a small terse noise from his throat. "I promised your mama if anything . . . I'd watch out for you. I don't know if I'm doing such a good job."

"It was good you brought me here, Ray."

I meant it, Mama.

"Anyhow, I talked to Bernice about you coming back with me at the end of the summer. Trixie's been after me to get a place, so . . . She's fixed it up real nice. You'd have a bedroom to yourself."

I felt like I was at the top of the roller coaster, waiting to swoop down to earth, fast. Ray was offering me the very thing I'd wanted all along. He continued talking while I held on tight. "I got a new job at the truck plant come September. I won't make as much money, but I'll be around more." He picked at one of his nails. "You think about it, is all. Okay?"

Now that Ray was offering to take me back, I wasn't sure I wanted to go. I didn't want to leave Aunt Bernie and Faith and Evangeline. They were my family too now.

"Just so you know, you always have a place. You can always come here for summers and holidays with Bernice."

I took a big breath.

"Ray, you've been like a daddy to me, and I don't want you to ever think I don't know it."

His John Deere hat shaded his eyes, leaving me in the dark as to what was in them.

"I promise to think hard about it."

"Okay, then." He got up and shuffled back and forth. Ray never could sit for long, could he, Mama?

"It's good to hear you talking again. Maybe one day you'll even lecture me a little bit, like you used to."

"You mean about you not smoking cigarettes and drinking beer, and about you eating something more than potato chips? You bet I will, Ray."

"Good." For the first time in a long time, he smiled, or what for Ray passed as smiling.

I sat up, determined to get at what was bugging me the most, Mama.

"Ray, Mama wasn't baking cookies that day, was she?"

His cheeks flushed red. All the things Ray had said before . . . I could see on his face that they were things he'd said to protect me, and that he still wanted to, badly.

He struggled for a moment, but then looked me right in the eye and told me what I already knew in my heart.

"No, honey, she wasn't."

We contemplated each other. All the things we needed to say couldn't have really been said anyway. Some things are best left that way. Unsaid, but understood.

Not wanting Ray to feel bad about his story, the first thing that popped into my head came out of my mouth. "Well, shoot, I don't like cookies much anyway."

Ray blinked hard, startled a bit. His mouth opened to say something. Then closed.

He snorted.

I snorted.

He said, "Me neither."

I swear, Mama, we laughed up a storm until tears rained.

34

h-e-a-v-e-n

heaven (n.)

the space surrounding or seeming to overarch the
earth, in which the sun, moon, and stars appear;
the dwelling place of God and his angels where the
blessed live after death; any place of great beauty;
a state of happiness

The next morning, after Ray's visit, there was an envelope waiting for me beside my plate of eggs, with
"Briarwood Academy" in the top left corner. Aunt Bernie
bustled around the kitchen, making a racket with pot and
pan reorganization. "Ray left that for you."

"Why didn't he just give it to me himself?"

She sat down. "He wasn't sure you should have it. He
gave me the choice whether or not to give it to you. In
case you were accepted, he didn't want to interfere with

what I might decide to do about it. Said it wasn't his place. If you didn't get the scholarship spot, he said he couldn't bear to see you disappointed."

"But why did *you* give it to me?"

"Because it's addressed to you." She got up and continued with her task.

I looked at that envelope, Mama, hoping I could see into it with X-ray eyes. I didn't want Aunt Bernie to watch me open it. I wasn't even sure I wanted to open it at all.

So I left it there right on the table. For three whole days.

I helped Aunt Bernie in the garden, helped her clean the bathrooms, and assisted making a tuna casserole for Mrs. Myers from church, who'd been laid up with some ailment or other. Faith came over. We took a blanket outside, sat in the sun, and listened to the radio while Aunt Bernie vacuumed.

The envelope sat there on the table, looming larger and larger, until it seemed to take up the whole world. I could practically hear it shout *OPEN ME!* even while I slept.

When Aunt Bernie gave me the go-ahead, and said I was well enough to ride Maybelle, I stuffed the envelope into my bag and headed out to town.

I rode to the gas station. Bean looked up and smiled his crooked-tooth grin when I came inside. "Well, look who's come to see old Bean." He came round the counter and gave me a good hard one-armed hug. "Glad to see you up and around." He put his hand on the top of my head. "You gave us a scare, kid."

"Bean," I began, nervous. I hoped he wasn't mad about me crossing over that fence.

"Why so serious, now?"

"I'm sorry I was trespassing, I really am. It's just so beautiful there, and the swans became like friends to me."

"Well, I can't think of anybody I'd rather have trespassing."

"I was wondering if it's okay if I still check on the swans. They're used to me coming, and I promise I won't go near the water again."

"If it's okay with Bernie, I'd have to say it's okay with me. I knew your mama my whole life. Heck, you're practically family."

Then I explained what I had in mind for you, Mama. He said he'd be pleased, and we shook on it.

I went out to my bike, but then stopped, Bean's words circling in my head, "*Heck, you're practically family.*" I hurried back inside before I thought twice about it.

"My goodness, girl, you got something else on your mind?"

"Bean, are you my daddy?"

Squinting hard, he surveyed me as if I'd lost my fool mind. Finally he leaned back in his chair and hooted at the ceiling.

"By God, you're serious. No, honey. I'm not your daddy. Your mama was too special for the likes of me. But I'll tell you what, I'd be mighty proud if I were."

I rode out to the swan's nest, a little disappointed about Bean not being the winner of the contest. He said he always figured it was this particular visiting college boy from Ohio State, the cousin of somebody or other, who'd worked at the feed store the summer Bean left for Vietnam.

"But if I hadn't been trudging through muck, carrying a rifle," he said, "your mama would never have had to leave Shepherdsville." Old Bean sounded as if he had been sweet on you too, Mama.

Then he sent me on my way. "Go on, now. Surely you got something better to do than jaw with me."

Bean had cleared a path to the pond. The weeds and long grasses had been mowed down to the ground. Mr. Cobb, who'd lost some feathers in the fight with Marlow, swam slowly, circling the cygnets, a bit wary of me. His neck was low, curled tight into himself. He finally settled on the bank, near the babies, their yellow-and-gray down having given way to more adult plumage.

Evangeline had said that swans mate for life and I should expect Mr. Cobb to mourn Penny, just like a human would. He might never take another partner to replace her. Some of Penny's white feathers lay scattered in the area by the nest. A few caught in the breeze and floated nearby. I plucked one from the ground and ran it across my cheek, letting its softness linger there. I tucked it into my bag, and my hands brushed against the envelope from Briarwood.

I crawled onto the tree limb. I closed my eyes and waited a bit. When I couldn't bear it any longer, I tore open the envelope and slowly pulled out the single sheet of paper. I unfolded it, holding my breath.

We are pleased to inform you that your application to Briarwood Academy has been accepted for the school year 1977–78 . . .

I clamped my hand over my mouth, but a squeal escaped anyway, agitating Mr. Cobb, who spread his wings in protest. "Sorry," I apologized. "Sorry."

But I couldn't help myself. I hollered out, "We did it, Mama!"

I hope you heard me.

Aunt Bernie didn't say anything about the envelope being missing. During supper she didn't mention it, or while we washed the dishes. Later she sat in front of the television watching the news, crocheting squares. I took a spot on the couch next to her.

Walter Cronkite was talking about the space shuttle *Enterprise* that flew for four whole minutes out in California. The film reel showed the shuttle riding on the back of an airliner, with two smaller air force jets flying alongside. There was something in their formation through the clouds that reminded me of the swans flying into the heavens. I thought of what Bean had said about that astronaut flying to heaven and saying he didn't see God up there. Maybe he didn't fly high enough, Mama.

Maybe one day I really will be able to take a shuttle right to you.

Aunt Bernie interrupted my thoughts. "Did you open it?"

I nodded.

"Did you get the scholarship?"

I nodded.

"Good. Do you want to go?"

I nodded.

"If it's what Emma wanted for you, then it's what I want for you too." I watched her crochet needle bob, in and out, making an intricate pattern out of a simple piece of yarn, never dropping a stitch.

Walter Cronkite signed off, "And that's the way it is. August 12, 1977."

35

m-e-t-a-m-o-r-p-h-o-s-i-s

metamorphosis (n.)

a change of form, shape, structure; transformation;
a marked or complete change of character; the form
resulting from such change

On my last afternoon in Shepherdsville, Aunt Bernie and I headed out to the end-of-summer church picnic, the final supper before crops and school called everybody to their tasks.

Ray and Trixie were expected to arrive and have a bite with us. Then I'd head off with them to get settled in before the school year began.

I had packed up my clothes in your suitcase, Mama, leaving my church dresses behind in the closet, tucked behind old moth-eaten coats. I had carefully folded up the map of the world from the wall in your old room and tucked it on top of my clothes. Aunt Bernie had said I could bring it with me if I liked.

My dictionary and spelling trophy went into a grocery bag. All the words I'd written and dropped into its cup were tucked into the pockets of my jeans. The box on the mantel had been the last thing I took before I left the farmhouse. Maybelle stayed in the barn, waiting for my return next summer.

I helped Aunt Bernie set up food on banquet tables that had been lugged up to the field next to the church. People arrived, mingling and surveying all the goodies, piling plates sky-high with barbecued chicken, potato salad, pies, cakes, casseroles, and watermelon.

Reverend Love and Mary entertained a long line of folks who gathered round hoping to hold Charity. Faith sat on a picnic table, huddled over her guitar. Jason, along with Matt, Missy, and Lerman, listened at her feet on the grass. Even Leann Shank and Loretta wandered over to join them.

Evangeline introduced her younger sister, Celeste, from Atlanta, who'd moved up to Shepherdsville to live with Evangeline for a while. Celeste had a laugh as deep and rich as Evangeline's.

"I hear you helped Evangeline to make this a more

colorful place, Dulcie." She giggled with Aunt Bernie. "Those robes! Aren't they something?"

Aunt Bernie caught Celeste's drift. "Well, I have to say, Len and Lou and the entire tenor section look divine in lavender."

Evangeline smiled, a bit wicked. "Don't they just?"

When everyone had settled, I got the box from Littleton Funeral Home out of Aunt Bernie's car, along with my Bible bag. Aunt Bernie saw me leave. We exchanged a glance across all the heads. She knew what I was off to do. She'd asked ahead of time if I wanted for her to come with me, but it was something I wanted to do by myself.

I walked along the fence line, the Bible bag thumping against my thigh, the Bible and the treasure I'd found in its pages a comforting weight as I walked.

You see, I hadn't been sure what I wanted to say, Mama, but I wanted the words to be right.

The night before, I'd thumbed through my dictionary, trying to find the right word—the last word—to give you before I left.

I'd even paged through Aunt Bernie's Bible, something I hadn't done much of since I'd arrived in Shepherdsville. After I'd finally settled on the one word that made sense, a small piece of yellowed paper folded into thirds had fallen out of the Bible, into my lap. When I opened it, I saw that it was in your handwriting, Mama.

It was the letter Aunt Bernie had told me about—the one you wrote her after you left Shepherdsville. After all this time, Mama, to have your words, to hear your voice as I read them, was to get you back for just a moment. I let my eyes travel the page, and they landed on my name.

. . . I call her Dulcie, which means "sweet," and she is. Promise me that if anything ever happens, you will watch over her, Bernie.

I hope you know, Mama, that Aunt Bernie kept her promise.

That last afternoon, out in the field behind the church, I climbed over Bean's repaired fence, using the split rails like a ladder. I made my way to the other side, careful not to drop the box. The sun was low in the sky, everything touched with gold light, sprinkling jewels of sparkles across the water. I watched the swans for a bit as they waltzed on the surface of the pond. I fed them bits of stashed cornbread wrapped in a napkin from the picnic. The cygnets grabbed the crumbs willy-nilly while Mr. Cobb looked on, swimming nearby, gliding, keeping watch. Evangeline warned me that when it was time for the cygnets to fly in the fall, they might not return—I might not see them again.

I held the box in front of me. You didn't have any kind of proper send-off, Mama. I wanted you to have a place of your own. The swan's pond is the most peaceful place I know of, and Bean said it would be all right with him. Evangeline's idea that everybody should have a place where they can visit and talk with their loved ones rang true to me.

But mostly I thought of the words you'd written in the letter to Aunt Bernie and how you'd said that the most important thing was forgiveness.

The best way I know how to love, Bernie, is simply to forgive.

I opened the Littleton Funeral Home box, then placed each word from my spelling cup into it. The very last word—the word I'd decided on the night before—was the word I whispered as I slid the box into the water. I stood at the edge of the pond, by the cattails and reeds, and watched the box disappear.

When I had almost drowned at the pond, something inside had made me fight and kick to rise to the surface. I see now how you were drowning too, Mama, and didn't have the fight anymore to rise up out of it. If the best way to love is to forgive, then I forgive you for not being able to save yourself.

Ray found me at the pond.

"Bernie told me you'd be back here." He looked around. "This is a good place. A real good place."

We stood silently for a moment, letting the sun dapple the water with shimmers. Then we headed back over the fence. Ray vaulted the split rails neatly. He took my hand to help me over, and then didn't let go. As we walked through the field, hand in hand, our feet swishing through the grass along the fence line, I could hear Faith singing, her voice carried on the breeze.

> *Down in the valley,*
> *Valley so low;*
> *Hang your head over,*
> *Hear the wind blow.*

Trixie and Ray waited in the car while I said my goodbyes. Faith did it quick, like she was yanking off a Band-Aid. She bumped my hip with hers. "See you in the funny papers."

She walked away, back to Reverend Love and Mary. She took the baby from Mary and waved Charity's little hand at me. Jason and the others waved from the field. Even Loretta.

Evangeline took my face in her hands but didn't say a word—she didn't need to.

As a surprise, Aunt Bernie and Evangeline gave me a quilt they'd made from crocheted squares and swatches of your old choir robe, Mama, to put on my new bed at Ray's place.

Aunt Bernie lugged a giant wicker picnic basket of food over and had Ray put it in the trunk.

"Aunt Bernie, that's too much food," I said.

"Well, it might have to last you until you come for Thanksgiving. Doesn't look to me like that Trixie can boil water. You're likely to starve to death."

She grabbed me and held me something fierce. She whispered into my ear, "You come back to me, you hear."

I slipped into the backseat. Reverend Love leaned in the window and said, "Take care." He slapped the roof of the car twice above my head.

As Ray drove down the pike, something made me turn around and look through the rear window. In the looming twilight, I could make out above the trees, behind the church, a swan sailing in the sky, wings outstretched, gliding and swooping, a line of cygnets practicing behind.

Mr. Cobb was teaching his babies how to fly.

I hoped what Reverend Love told me was true, Mama—that swans ferry souls to heaven. That is my true prayer.

Amen.

That was the last word that went into the box with you—the only fitting word I could find in Aunt Bernie's Bible.

"Amen."

Webster's definition: "May it be so! May it be so!"

I watched until the swans disappeared from view. Then I turned and faced the road ahead.

Acknowledgments

I am incredibly thankful to Beach Lane Books, and to all those who contributed their marvelous assistance, reading, and guidance. Heartfelt gratitude goes to my endlessly supportive editor, Allyn Johnston, for her extraordinary faith in this book.

Many thanks to Aimée Bissonette for insight and advice.

I owe a particular debt to the kindred spirits, fellow writers, and faculty of the MFAC program of Hamline University, especially Jane Resh Thomas, who allowed me to believe I could write the map of my heart, and Gary D. Schmidt, for encouraging me to see what was on the other side of the fence.

My deepest appreciation to my Ohio family for providing inspiration for this book and lighting the path home, particularly to my brothers, Mark and Joe, for walking alongside me.

And most of all, my love and thanks to my husband, Steven, and to my children, Remmer and Sophie, for the gift of their belief and enthusiasm. Thank you for standing under the vast starry sky and wishing with me.

If you or someone you know needs help, call 1-800-273-8255 for the National Suicide Prevention Lifeline. You can also text HOME to 741741 for free, 24-hour support from the Crisis Text Line.